"What if you were to discover that your sister's fiancé is attracted to you?"

"Don't say that," Kate groaned.

Gabriel's eyes moved over her. He had to admit that he didn't understand what he was feeling. This was the twin sister of the woman who was making his life a living hell and threatening his only child. And all he could think about was pulling her into his arms and kissing her until neither of them could think straight.

"I wish," he said quietly, "that we could have met under different circumstances."

"But we didn't…and I think we should spend as little time together as possible between now and the wedding."

"You know that won't change anything." Without saying another word, Gabriel walked away from her.

Kate, her heart hammering, watched until he was out of sight. She was just going to have to stay away from him….

Dear Reader,

Happy New Year! I hope this year brings you all your heart desires…and I hope you enjoy the many books coming your way this year from Silhouette Special Edition!

January features an extraspecial THAT SPECIAL WOMAN!—Myrna Temte's *A Lawman for Kelly*. Deputy U.S. Marshal Steve Anderson is back (remember him in Myrna's *Room for Annie?*), and he's looking for love in Montana. Don't miss this warm, wonderful story!

Then travel to England this month with *Mistaken Bride*, by Brittany Young—a compelling Gothic story featuring two identical twins with very different personalities…. Or stay at home with *Live-In Mom* by Laurie Paige, a tender story about a little matchmaker determined to bring his stubborn dad to the altar with the right woman! And don't miss *Mr. Fix-It* by Jo Ann Algermissen. A man who is good around the house is great to find anytime during the year!

This month also brings you *The Lone Ranger*, the initial story in Sharon De Vita's winsome new series, SILVER CREEK COUNTY. Falling in love is all in a day's work in this charming Texas town. And watch for the first book by a wonderful writer who is new to Silhouette Special Edition—Neesa Hart. Her book, *Almost to the Altar*, is sure to win many new fans.

I hope this New Year shapes up to be the best year ever! Enjoy this book, and all the books to come!

Sincerely

Tara Gavin
Senior Editor

Please address questions and book requests to:
Silhouette Reader Service
U.S.: 3010 Walden Ave., P.O. Box 1325, Buffalo, NY 14269
Canadian: P.O. Box 609, Fort Erie, Ont. L2A 5X3

BRITTANY YOUNG
MISTAKEN BRIDE

Published by Silhouette Books
America's Publisher of Contemporary Romance

SILHOUETTE BOOKS

ISBN 0-373-24076-7

MISTAKEN BRIDE

Books by Brittany Young

BRITTANY YOUNG

lives and writes in Racine, Wisconsin. She has traveled to most of the countries that serve as the settings for her books and finds the research into the language, customs, history and literature of these countries among the most demanding and rewarding aspects of her writing.

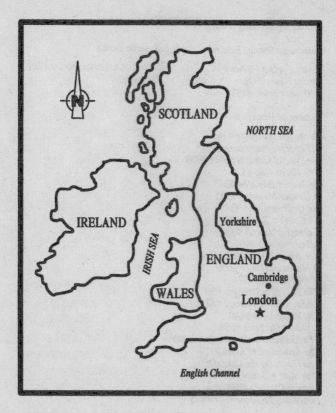

Prologue

The two little girls, seven years old and best friends, had just come out of the house into the sunny yard and were talking, trying to decide what to do with their day. The one who lived in the house, Kate Fairfax, was a striking child, tall for her age with auburn hair and smoky blue eyes. Her friend Jane, blond and petite, said something that sent them both into peals of infectious laughter.

Kate's identical twin came running out of the house, whipped a cupcake out from behind her back and gleefully showed it to the two girls. "Want a bite?"

Kate looked at her sister with serious eyes. "Carly, Mom said we couldn't have one until after dinner."

Carly defiantly bit into the cupcake. "So?"

"You'll get into trouble."

"I don't care." Carly, who was looking over her sister's shoulder toward the house, suddenly blanched and shoved the cupcake into Kate's hand.

"I told you I don't want any."

And then Kate heard their mother's voice as she strode toward them. "All right," she said angrily, "which one of you took it?"

Carly looked pleadingly at her sister and Kate resigned herself to what was about to happen.

The woman planted herself in front of her daughters. It had been a long day and she was at the end of her rope. She grabbed the cupcake from Kate's hand and dashed it to the ground. "Didn't I say that you couldn't have one until after dinner?"

"Yes, ma'am," said Kate.

"And you took one anyway. Why?"

Kate said nothing.

"Well?" said her mother impatiently.

Kate lifted her thin shoulders. "I guess I was hungry."

She grabbed Kate by the upper arms and shoved her toward the house. "You're going to be a lot hungrier. Go straight to your room and stay there until tomorrow morning." She swatted Kate on the bottom for good measure as they walked up the steps and into the house.

Jane glared at Carly. "Why don't you tell your mom who really took it?"

Carly pulled a face. She couldn't stand Jane. "Why don't you mind your own business?"

Jane had seen this happen time and again. Carly misbehaved and Kate took the blame. She didn't know whom to be angrier at—Carly for taking advantage of her sister's protective nature or Kate for allowing it. Jane might only be seven, but she knew it was wrong.

Kate went to her room, quietly closed the door and sat on the window seat near her canopied bed, her arms wrapped around her legs, her cheek on her knees, as she gazed outside.

Jane raised her hand as she stood on the lawn looking up sadly at her friend. Kate pressed her own palm against the window in response. Sometimes she wished she could just go home with Jane. Her family was so normal, so nice. Her house was always filled with delicious smells and the laughter of a big family. Kate's own home seemed to have lost all of its joy the day her father had walked out three years ago. He'd never come back and her mother had seemed angry ever since. Jane's parents had offered to let Kate stay with them last year. Kate desperately wanted to, and she even thought her mother might allow it—but she couldn't bring herself to leave her twin.

Kate loved her sister, but she wasn't blind to her faults. She knew, in the intuitive way children did, that despite Carly's bravado, she was really very weak. So Kate had appointed herself her twin's protector. It was a responsibility she took very seriously.

Carly, standing beside Jane, looked up at Kate, her expression contrite. But as she turned away from the house, her back to her sister, her mouth twitched into a smile.

Chapter One

Even with the scar that etched its way down the length of his cheek, the man with the shoulder-length dark hair was strikingly handsome. And very angry.

He paced from one end of his attorney's London office to the other. "We've got to be able to do something. This Carly Fairfax woman can't come into my life out of nowhere and threaten that she'll take my daughter away from me unless I marry her."

"Willa is her biological daughter, Gabriel."

"A daughter whom she gave up for adoption years ago to my late wife and me."

"True."

"What are my options?" he asked as he came to an abrupt stop in front of the desk.

"At this point, Gabriel, the only thing you can do is legally protect every asset you have before the marriage to make sure she can't get her hands on anything when you divorce her."

"She doesn't want my money, Harry. If that's what she was after, she would have taken it when I offered it to her."

"I suppose that's true."

"So what does she get out of marriage to me?"

"What she says she wants and what the reality is is anyone's guess. I personally think it's your name and social position, even though she claims the marriage is the best way to provide Willa with a stable home."

"I've watched her with Willa, Harry. She doesn't care about her welfare. She barely acknowledges the child's existence. There's something else going on. And it doesn't have anything to do with my name or social position. I may be well-known as an architect, but she's equally well-known as a model. And as for social position, that belonged to my father, not to me."

The attorney shrugged his dark-suited shoulders. "Apparently she has her own agenda."

Gabriel's face showed his frustration. "You're a lawyer. Can't you fix this? Isn't there something we can do?"

"How this gets fixed is entirely up to you, Gabriel. If you force her hand and deny her what she wants, which is marriage to you, then she might well follow through on her threat to take the child away."

"Willa was legally adopted when she was a week old. You know that. You handled it, for God's sake."

"I know." The attorney looked away from Gabriel as he uncomfortably shuffled some papers on his desk. "We did everything by the book, you can be sure of that."

"Then how can a court possibly take her away from me now, six years later?"

"We don't know for certain that they will, of course, but there's always that risk. When you adopted Willa, you were married. The child came into a two-parent home. When your wife died, everything changed. All the court has to do is decide that Willa would be better off with her biological mother rather than her adoptive father and that will be the end of it. You read the papers, Gabriel. You know that adoptive parents— even the married ones—are losing their children to the biological parents. It doesn't happen every time, of course, but it happens often enough to give one pause."

"We can't let this get to court."

"The problem is that it will if you don't marry this woman and she follows through with her threat."

Gabriel dragged his fingers through his thick, dark hair. "She's got me in a corner I can't get out of. My choice is no choice at all."

"That's right. Unless you're willing to assume the risk of losing your daughter."

"I'm not." Gabriel walked to the window and stared outside. "So that's it."

"Of course, you could always hire someone to bump her off," the attorney said with a mild attempt at humor. "That would certainly solve your problem."

Gabriel didn't respond. He hadn't found humor in anything since Carly Fairfax had shown up on his doorstep.

The attorney cleared his throat. "Anyway, I'll get together with your accountant to make sure all of your assets are protected in such a way as to be untouchable by this woman. I understand that's not your primary concern at the moment, but you'll appreciate it when it comes time for the divorce."

Gabriel turned away from the window, his expression grim and unreadable. "I appreciate your help, Harry."

"I wish I could do more," he said as he rose from his chair and walked around the desk. "Does your grandmother know what's going on?"

"Unfortunately, yes. She overheard an argument."

"What was her reaction?"

A corner of Gabriel's mouth lifted. "She was her usual practical self. She said I should go ahead and marry the woman and, as soon as Willa is of legal age, divorce her and get on with my life."

"What about your brother?"

"Richard? He's oblivious to everything but himself, although he seems to have developed something of a crush on the Fairfax woman. No one else on my end knows, nor do I want them to."

"What about the woman's family? What's the level of their involvement?"

"I only know what the detectives found. It's all in the report you gave me. Her father left when she was small. She has a twin sister she's in occasional touch with and a mother she hasn't kept in touch with at all. I suppose if she's told anyone, it would be the sister.''

"This is all very unfortunate.''

"I don't want Willa to find out accidentally or otherwise what's going on. She's known she's adopted, but she doesn't need to know about this woman's threat to take her away from the only home she's ever known. She's had enough to deal with in her young life.''

"I understand.''

"I'd appreciate it if you'd lock up the file, Harry. I don't even want your secretary to have access. If I have to marry this woman to keep Willa, that's what I'm going to do. But no one else needs to know.''

"Consider it done.''

"Thank you, Harry. You're a good friend.'' He sighed. "I wish I knew how she found out where Willa was. The adoption records are supposed to be sealed.''

"It's easy to get information if you're determined enough.''

"I suppose.''

The attorney reached out a hand and firmly clasped Gabriel's strong shoulder. The two of them had been friends since childhood. Their homes were only a few miles apart. He'd always admired and respected Gabriel. "I wish I could do more.''

"I know, Harry, but you can't. Whatever happens from this point forward will be up to me.''

"When is the ceremony supposed to take place?''

"One month.'' He looked at the attorney for a long moment. "Unless something happens to change the situation,'' he said quietly.

Harry nodded.

* * *

The woman, her long auburn hair brushed away from her beautiful face into a neat ponytail, sat at her desk in a cramped office on the third floor of the Chicago art museum, staring blankly out the window.

Another woman poked her head around the open door and tapped on the door frame. "Katie? Are you ready to go to lunch?"

Kate swivelled her chair around and smiled at her friend. "I'm sorry, Jane. I should have met you downstairs but I lost track of time."

Jane came farther into the office. "What's wrong?"

Kate picked up a yellow sheet of paper and handed it to her. "Read this."

Jane's eyes scanned the top. "A telegram? I didn't even know people sent these things any longer."

"Carly does, particularly if she doesn't want to talk to me on the phone."

Jane quickly read the message, a frown deepening the creases in her forehead. "This is so Carly. She wants you to drop everything and fly to England but doesn't tell you why."

"She's probably in trouble."

"With her track record, I'd say that's a good bet." She handed back the telegram. "Are you going to go?"

"I think I have to."

"You could ignore it."

"She's my sister. Since Carly and Mom fell out all those years ago, I'm her only family."

Jane sighed. "It's just like when we were children. Carly misbehaves and you run to the rescue."

"She'd do the same for me if it was necessary."

Jane arched an expressive brow.

"I'm sure she would," said Kate defensively.

"Yeah, well, I wouldn't put it to the test. Carly looks out for Carly, and that's the way it's always been."

"She isn't strong like we are."

Jane grabbed Kate's hand and pulled her out of her chair. "Come on, let's get some lunch. I refuse to get into another argument with you over your sister. You've always worn blinders where she's concerned."

Kate took her purse out of her bottom desk drawer and slid the strap over her shoulder. "That's not true. I'm aware of her faults."

"And you forgive her for every one of them."

"She can't help the way she is."

"Any more than you can help the way you are." Jane looked into her dearest friend's eyes. "Katie, I know you mean well, but did it ever occur to you that you might be doing her more harm than good by bailing her out every time she asks for help?"

"Yes," said Kate quietly, "it's occurred to me often."

"And?"

"She's my only sister. I can't not go to her when she needs me."

"All right," said Jane with a wave of her hand. "End of discussion. Just let me know when you're leaving and call me when you get back. I don't need to know about anything in between. Now let's go. I'm starving and I have to be back in my bookstore in forty minutes."

* * *

Kate paced impatiently back and forth on the walkway outside the little airport while she waited for her twin. She had no idea what was going on. She didn't even have a number to call.

She was so worried she'd barely slept a wink for two days.

Now, here she was, in a small English town she'd never heard of, standing outside one of the tiniest airports she'd ever seen, waiting.

Jane was right, thought Kate. Coming here was a mistake. Who even knew if Carly would show up?

She'd been there for more than an hour when she finally spotted her sister roaring toward her in a bright red sports car with the top down.

Carly stopped in front of her twin with a squeal of tires, leaped out and dramatically threw her arms around Kate. "I would have been here sooner, but I was unavoidably tied up. Things have gotten so hectic over the past few weeks."

Kate couldn't help smiling. It was so typical of Carly to be careless about time. Particularly other people's. "If that's an apology, I grudgingly accept."

"I knew you wouldn't mind." Carly's eyes moved over her twin's pale skin and tired blue eyes. "You look beat. And those clothes!" She eyed Kate's rumpled, loose-fitting, cream-colored trousers, tucked-in blouse and the wide belt cinching her slender waist. "You have such a good figure, but you're always hiding it."

Kate was still amused as she looked at Carly's short, low-cut, formfitting red dress that left nothing to the imagination. "That's clearly not one of your problems."

"Like it?" asked Carly as she did a little turn, clearly pleased with herself.

"You're probably one of four women in the world who can pull off wearing something like that," said Kate dryly.

"True enough. That's why I get the big modelling bucks."

Kate grew more serious. "So what's going on? Your telegram sounded frantic. Are you in trouble?"

"Why is it that every time I contact you, you immediately assume I'm in trouble?"

"Because you usually are."

"Well, not this time." Carly couldn't cover her resentment. "I didn't ask you here to bail me out of anything."

"Then what's going on?"

Carly held up her left hand. A huge diamond ring sparkled in the sunlight.

Kate gently grasped Carly's hand and held it while she looked at the ring. "Oh, Carly, it's stunning. You're engaged?"

"To the most glorious, wonderful man in the world." She smiled at her sister. "He is incredibly handsome. And he's the first man I've really loved since Jeff."

What little color there was drained from Kate's cheeks.

Carly saw her reaction and gloried in it. "If you hadn't gotten pregnant, Jeff would have married me."

"Jeff has been dead for six years," said Kate tightly, "as has our child. So drop it, Carly."

"Sure. I just want the record straight on that one point."

"Straight? I'll tell you what's straight. You and Jeff never had a relationship. You never dated. You didn't even know Jeff until six months after I started seeing him."

"He slept with me."

"I don't believe you. He wouldn't have done that."

"He wanted *me,* Kate. He just didn't know how to tell you."

Kate put up her hand to silence her sister. "That's it. I'm not going to put myself through this. You asked me to come here and I came. Now I'm going to leave." As she turned away, Carly caught her arm.

"Don't, Katie. I'm sorry. I don't know what gets into me at times. Jeff is the past. This is very much the present. I wanted you here to share my joy, not to bring you grief. Forgive me?"

Kate closed her eyes.

"Please?"

With a sigh, Kate turned to face her sister.

"Come on. You know you love me."

A corner of Kate's mouth lifted. "You drive me crazy."

"I know. I don't mean to. And I promise I'll be good for the rest of your visit. Cross my heart. So stay, all right? I can't have a wedding without the most important person in my life being here."

Kate didn't answer. A feeling of the most enormous dread had come over her. A feeling she couldn't explain. A wedding was supposed to be a happy thing.

"Please?"

Still, she had always been there when Carly needed her. This was no different. "All right. I'll stay. But not too long. I'm using my vacation time to come here."

Carly hugged her. "I knew I could count on you."

"That's me. Good old reliable Kate." She picked up her sister's hand and looked at the ring again. "So when did all of this happen?"

"It was incredibly sudden. I was seeing his brother at first. He brought me here six weeks ago, and the moment Gabriel and I laid eyes on each other, that was it."

"What about his poor brother?"

"Richard? He'll get over it. You might even say this is a bit of a payback, considering the number of broken hearts he's left behind."

"Interesting way of looking at it."

Carly smiled.

"Did you say six weeks? Is that all the time you've known each other?"

"Katie, we knew what we wanted from the first moment."

"And you're happy?"

"Happier than I've ever been."

Kate hugged her twin. "I'm glad for you."

Carly hugged her back. "Who would have thought I'd be the first one of us to marry and start a family?"

Kate leaned back and looked at her sister. "A family? Are you . . . ?"

"No!" she said with a laugh. "But Gabriel has a daughter named Willa. She's six. Instant family."

"If he has a child, then he no doubt once had a wife."

Carly nodded. "Stephanie. She died a long time ago, so she's not going to be like a problem ex-wife."

Kate let that remark go. "Are you sure you want to take on the responsibility of a child and husband both at the same time?"

"I don't have a choice. It's a package deal. But I confess that my primary focus at the moment is becoming Mrs. Gabriel Trent."

Kate's eyes widened. "Gabriel Trent? The man you've been telling me about is Gabriel Trent, the architect?"

"You've heard of him?"

"Who hasn't? He's designed some of the most beautiful buildings in the world."

"I don't know anything about his work. He keeps an office at the house but he doesn't talk about it."

"And his grandfather was Lord William Trent, one of the best architects of his time."

"How do you know so much."

"At the museum, we deal with all forms of art, including architecture. Gabriel Trent is a legend. He's only in his thirties and books have already been written about him."

Carly beamed. "And he's all mine."

"I'm really looking forward to meeting him."

Carly's smile faded. "About that. Listen, he's a very reserved man in public. He's not one to show his affection. In fact, he might even come off as a little brusque, even with me. So don't pay too much attention to that. It's just his nature."

"A lot of geniuses are like that."

"I wouldn't know. He's the first one I've dated."

Kate smiled at her sister, relief evident in her eyes. "You have no idea how worried I was. I spent a flight across the Atlantic and another one from London to this place with my stomach in a knot."

"I'm sorry. I should have told you on the phone I had good news. Then you could have enjoyed your trip more. The important thing, though, is that you're here now. I want you to be part of the wedding preparations. And most of all, I want you to be my maid of honor. Will you?"

"Of course I will. You know how much I want to see you settled and happy." Kate paused for a moment, then asked the difficult question. "Are you inviting Mom?"

Carly grew instantly cool. "No."

"It's been so long since the two of you have spoken. I know she wants to be a part of your life again. This would be a wonderful way of starting over."

"I won't have her here. She would ruin everything. This is my wedding, and I'm going to do it the way I want and invite whomever I want—and not invite whomever I don't want."

Kate backed down. "I had to ask."

She had no idea what had split Carly and their mother apart. Neither of them would discuss it with her. But it must have been something terrible for the anger to have lasted this long. Once again Kate changed the subject. "When is the wedding?"

The storm cloud passed from Carly's face and was replaced with excitement. "Ten days." She looked at her watch. "Speaking of which, I'm late for my gown fitting. We'd better get moving." She looked at Kate's carry-on bag. "Where's the rest of your luggage?"

"It disappeared somewhere between Chicago and London. The airline put a trace on it. They said they'd send it here when they find it."

"So this is it?"

"Everything."

She tossed Kate's carry-on bag onto the back seat of her convertible and walked around to the driver's side. "Don't worry about your luggage. You can use my clothes until yours arrive."

Carly, always late and always in a hurry, gunned the engine before Kate had completely closed her door. With an amused shake of her head, Kate quickly snapped her seat belt securely into place. "I see you still drive too fast."

"You think I do everything too fast." She had to yell over the sound of the wind whipping their hair.

"You do!"

Carly laughed as she changed gears and drove even faster.

The little airport was in the middle of nowhere. The narrow two-lane highway leading away from it snaked through the countryside, past a small village and leisurely grazing cows.

Kate took a deep breath. "I smell the sea," she yelled to Carly.

"It'll come into view in a minute," she yelled back.

And suddenly it was there, a hundred feet below where they drove, an expanse of deep blue-black reaching all the way to the horizon, broken only by the whitecaps of the waves.

The road went from mildly winding to hairpin turns that were perilously close to the edge of the cliff as they made their way ever upward. "Carly," said Kate nervously, "I think you should slow down."

Carly went even faster. "You've always been afraid of anything even the least bit risky. Live a little!"

"What I'd like to do is live longer." The tires squealed as their edges clung to the road. Kate was genuinely frightened. "Slow down, Carly. I mean it!"

Carly reluctantly took her foot off the accelerator and downshifted. "You're no fun."

"That's the curse of those with common sense."

Carly downshifted again. "Cliff House is around the next bend."

"Cliff House?"

"My new home. You'll be able to see why it's called that in a few minutes."

And she did. As they turned down the long, winding driveway, the house suddenly came into view. It was a masterpiece of design, somehow blending in with the cliffs it stood watch over and every bit as angular. It even seemed to be built of the same stone as the cliffs. "It's huge," said Kate aloud.

"I hate it."

"Why?"

"It's depressing," said Carly as she parked in front of it. "I plan on spending as little time here as possible after the wedding."

Kate climbed out of the car, her eyes still on the mansion. "I like it. It's exactly the kind of place I'd expect Gabriel Trent to live."

"What if I were to tell you that there are people who actually believe the place is haunted?"

Kate's practical nature rebelled against such nonsense. "You're joking."

"Not at all."

"Haunted by whom? Or is it what?" Kate frowned. "Are ghosts *whom*s or *what*s?"

"*Whom*s, I suppose. And the *whom*s in this instance are three fishermen who were dashed against the cliffs one stormy night over sixty years ago when the lighthouse that used to sit on this spot failed to warn them." She reached into the back seat for Kate's bag and shoved it toward her sister. "Katie, I hate to do this to you, but I'm late for my fitting. Just go on into the house, introduce yourself to whoever's there and ask them to show you where your room is."

"But Carly..."

"Sorry. Gotta go."

Kate managed to grab her bag just as Carly gunned the engine and shot out of the circular driveway. Some things never changed, thought Kate as she walked up the steps to the huge door, lifted the brass knocker and let it fall.

A young and very handsome man who looked to be in his late twenties opened the door and grinned at her. "I was wondering where you were," he said in a very American accent as he put his arm around her waist and pulled her body against his.

Before Kate could say a word, she found herself in the middle of a passionate kiss. She dropped her bag and pushed her hands against his chest.

"I love it when you fight me," he whispered against her mouth.

"I'm not—" she managed to get out before his mouth was back on hers.

Kate lifted her high-heeled foot and brought it firmly down on top of his.

"Ow!" he yelled as he jumped back and glared at her. "What the hell is wrong with you?"

"What's wrong is that I'm not Carly."

He looked at her as though she'd lost her mind. "Now what game are you playing?"

"It's no game, I assure you. My name is Kate Fairfax. Carly and I are twins."

The man laughed.

Kate's gaze was steady, unsmiling.

The man's smile faded. "You're not kidding, are you?"

"No."

"What can I say? I'm really sorry."

"It's an understandable mistake," said Kate as she straightened her blouse.

He stepped toward her with an outstretched hand. "Let's start over. Hello, Kate. I'm Richard Trent."

Kate looked at him in surprise. "Richard?"

"That's right."

"You're not her fiancé?"

He had the grace to look embarrassed. "Not quite the greeting you'd expect from a prospective brother-in-law, I know."

"Not quite," she agreed.

"Don't get the wrong idea," said Richard. "It was a joke, nothing more."

That kiss was no joke. It was the kiss of a man who expected a response.

Richard, a frown deepening the lines on the bridge between his eyes, took a step toward Kate and looked closely at her, feature by feature. "It's amazing. You look exactly like her."

"That's usually the case with identical twins," she said unsmilingly. She hadn't met Gabriel yet, but already she was feeling protective toward him. And angry with Carly for whatever was apparently still going on between her and this man.

"Carly just said she had a sister. She didn't say anything about a twin, identical or otherwise." He continued to stare. "I can't get over it." He reached out to touch her hair.

"May I come the rest of the way inside?" asked Kate, still standing on the stoop.

"Oh, of course," he said with a friendly smile as he stepped aside. "I'm sorry."

Kate felt really awkward. She wondered if Carly had bothered to tell anyone she was coming.

Richard picked up her oversize shoulder bag. "Is this all of your luggage?"

"All that made it to England."

He shook his head. "I can't get over it. You even sound like her. Are you a model, too?"

The foyer was large and square with a tiled floor and a glass cathedral ceiling that soared more than three stories above their heads. Sunlight poured in through the glass in long, visible beams. The foyer itself was large, open and uncluttered. It was stunning. "No. My interests took me in another direction."

"So what do you do?"

"I'm an acquisitions director at a museum in Chicago."

"Sounds...interesting."

His voice said it was anything but interesting. Kate couldn't help smiling. "I enjoy it."

"But no modelling?"

"You're a little one-track on this modelling thing."

"I like models."

"So do I. I just don't happen to be one."

"All right. Consider me off the track."

"Thank you." Kate looked around. "Should I stay here and wait for Carly to get back from her fitting?"

"No, of course not. The fact that I didn't know you were coming doesn't mean anything. I rarely know what's going on around here. If Carly told anyone, it would be Mrs. Peabody." He took her hand and pulled her along behind him. "I think I know where she is."

"Who's Mrs. Peabody?"

"The housekeeper."

Of course a place like this would have a housekeeper.

They walked into the kitchen. There was a woman bent over, looking into a cabinet.

"Mrs. Peabody?" said Richard.

As she straightened and turned toward them, Kate saw an attractive woman in her fifties—perhaps early sixties—with a lovely face, beautiful skin, friendly eyes and a warm smile. That smile embraced Richard, but when her gaze got to Kate, it grew noticeably cooler.

Richard went to the woman, kissed her on the cheek and wrapped his arm around her shoulders. "Drop the chill, Mrs. Peabody. This is Carly's sister, Kate. Did you know she was coming?"

She didn't bother to smile this time as she eyed Kate. "Yes. Miss Fairfax asked me to prepare a room."

"And did you?"

She looked up at Richard and frowned as she affectionately slapped his hand off her shoulder. "Of course."

"Which one?"

"Never you mind," she said in a strong accent that Kate couldn't place. "I'll show her myself." She walked past Kate. "If you please, follow me, Miss Fairfax."

Kate grabbed her shoulder bag from Richard and obediently followed Mrs. Peabody.

The housekeeper was ramrod straight and cooly silent as she led Kate back to the foyer and up the elegantly curved, tiled staircase that led to the second floor.

"Your sister asked that you be placed in the room next to hers," said the woman as she turned right down a long and very wide, lavishly Oriental-carpeted hallway.

"This is your sister's room," she said as they passed an ornately carved door. "And this is yours." She opened a door just down the hall and stepped aside for her to enter. "If you need anything, ask. We're not mind readers."

"Thank you."

"Excuse me, please," she said, her voice as cold as her demeanor. "I have other duties to which I must attend."

"Of course you do. I appreciate your taking the time to—" The door closed firmly behind Mrs. Peabody before Kate could finish her sentence.

If her first two encounters were anything to go by, this visit was going to be an interesting experience.

Kate put her shoulder bag on the bed, walked to the windows and opened the drapes to let the sunshine in, pulling back one heavy panel and then the other to expose huge windows and a view of the sea that was nothing short of spectacular. She searched for window latches and found them near the center. Standing on her toes, she undid them, then pulled the windows toward her to open them the way one would double doors. A strong, cool breeze off the sea immediately filled the room. Kate leaned outside and let the wind whip her hair. She loved her work, but one of the disadvantages was that it kept her cooped up. She'd love to wake up to this every morning.

Gabriel walked along the cliffs, as he often did when he needed to think. He pushed his dark hair away from his face, but the wind blew it right back.

He didn't notice.

Stopping about fifty yards from his home, he leaned his shoulder against the trunk of a tree, strong arms across his chest, and gazed at the sea.

It was fairly calm today. Almost peaceful. But Gabriel liked the sea best when it raged, slamming into the cliffs below and creating a deafening roar.

He turned his head slightly, his eyes moving over his house.

That's when he saw her leaning out of the window.

His already serious expression hardened.

Never in his life had he hated anyone the way he hated Carly Fairfax. And in less than two weeks, he was going to be married to her.

The muscle in his jaw tightened.

Kate, completely unaware of the mess she was in the middle of, pulled her head back inside the room and looked around. The room was large and open, furnished plainly, with simple taste and straight lines with an occasional piece of ornateness that caught the eye but didn't overwhelm it. She knew fine furniture, and this was definitely the best that money could buy. She wondered if Gabriel had designed it himself, as he frequently did for many of his buildings.

And to think he was going to be a member of her family.

Taking a brush out of her bag, she ran it through her long auburn hair, pulling it back into a ponytail that she fastened with a rubber band. A few strands of shorter hair in the front still framed her pale oval face and set off her smoky blue eyes with their luxuriant fringe of dark lashes. She had finally grown into the lips that had seemed too full in childhood. The lipstick she'd put on hours earlier had worn away without a trace, but she didn't bother to freshen it.

There were no clean clothes to change into, so showering was pointless. And there wasn't a chance that she'd be able to sleep. Reaching into her bag, she pulled out a pair of comfortable loafers and slipped into them, then left her room to go exploring.

Running down the steps like a child rather than a woman of twenty-five, she went straight out the door she'd come in earlier and walked around the front of the house to the cliff side. With her hands jammed in the pockets of her trousers, she crossed the hundred feet from the house to the cliffs and stood on the edge, looking out at the vast sea and its waves of midnight blue capped with white. The jagged cliffs dropped straight down for more than a hundred and fifty feet, but then developed a more gentle angle before meeting the sea.

As Kate stood there, she gradually became aware that she wasn't alone. Someone was watching her.

Even as she had the thought, Kate felt someone close behind her. So close she could feel the heat from his body. Kate wanted to turn, but it was as though she was frozen in place.

A mouth moved close to her ear. "It's dangerous to stand so close to the edge," said a deep voice. "You might lose your balance." His body crowded hers, pressing her closer to the edge of the cliff. She couldn't turn. She couldn't fight. There was no room.

A strong arm suddenly went around her waist and pulled her back until she was pressed against a solid wall of chest. "See what I mean?"

Kate turned within the circle of that arm, frighteningly well aware that if he let go, she'd tumble backward off the cliff. She found herself looking into a pair of cold, tawny eyes. Her heart sank. This was a man who was capable of killing her. She knew it. She could see it.

It would be so easy, thought Gabriel. All he'd have to do is let go, and his problem would be solved. No more threats. No more blackmail. No more marriage.

He looked into her frightened, pleading eyes. She knew she was helpless. She knew it was his decision and his alone as to whether she would live or die.

His arm tightened around her waist.

Chapter Two

"Gabriel? Kate?" called Richard as he crossed the lawn toward them.

Gabriel stared at her, long and hard. The muscle in his jaw tightened. "Kate?"

Her heart hammered against her ribs. "Yes," she said breathlessly. "I'm Carly's twin sister."

As quickly as that, his grip on her eased. He pulled her away from the cliff and steadied Kate on her wobbly legs.

"What's going on?" asked Richard as he approached.

Gabriel was still holding her. "She was standing too close to the edge of the cliff. I was afraid she'd fall, so I pulled her back."

"You can't be too careful," said Richard. "Sometimes the unexpected wind gusts around here can knock you off your feet."

"You're shaking," said Gabriel, still focused on Kate.

She couldn't take her eyes from him. "Near-death experiences have a tendency to affect me that way."

"You're fine now. Just remember not to get so close to the edge in the future."

Kate nodded, wondering how she could possibly have so completely misunderstood what had happened. If he was saving her, why had she felt so threatened?

She watched Gabriel as he walked away. That was ridiculous. He had thought she was Carly, the woman he loved. Of course he wouldn't hurt her.

Richard touched her shoulder. Kate was so intent on Gabriel that she'd forgotten he was there, and she swung around and screamed at the top of her lungs.

Richard was so startled that he tripped when he stepped back and fell on the ground. "What the hell is wrong with you?" he asked as he looked up at her in astonishment.

Kate was so relieved she laughed. "I'm sorry." She stretched out her hand to help him up. "You startled me."

"Apparently. Thanks." He dusted off his pants. "Next time I'll poke you with a stick to get your attention."

Kate was still preoccupied. She turned toward where she'd last seen Gabriel. "What was your brother doing out here?"

"Gabriel haunts the cliffs—especially when he's working on a design. He claims they help him think."

"Do they?"

He shrugged. "Who knows? Personally I can take them or leave them. Kate?"

"Mm-hmm?"

"Hello? Are you listening?"

She turned toward him with a smile. "I'm sorry. What?"

"We got off to a bad start earlier. I'm sorry. It was completely my fault. I had no business behaving like that."

"I wasn't going to bring it up," she said, "but since you did, what exactly were you doing kissing my sister that way?"

"Technically I was kissing you."

"But you thought I was Carly."

He shrugged. "I have no defense. I'm a cad. And I find your sister to be a very attractive woman."

"A very attractive woman who happens to be engaged to your brother."

"True."

"So why would you kiss her like that?"

"I felt like it."

"Do you always do what you feel like?"

"If you're here long enough to get to know me, Kate, what you'll discover is that I'm a man of many charms and few morals. If I'm attracted to a woman and she's attracted to me, nothing else matters. I don't care if she's married—or engaged—to my brother."

"That's really sad," said Kate. "You must be very unhappy."

He lifted a dark brow. "Hardly."

"One of these days," said Kate, "you're going to truly fall in love. Then you'll realize what you've been playing at."

He smiled at her, his eyes moving over her face. "Maybe I'll fall in love with you."

"If you're attracted to my sister, I can assure you that you won't be attracted to me. Our personalities are as different as our appearances are alike."

Richard nodded slowly. "I can see that."

Kate rubbed her hands up and down on her arms. "I think I'm going to go inside. It's chilly out here."

"Oh!" said Richard, "believe it or not, I came out here for a reason. There's a party this evening at a neighbor's house. Carly said she neglected to mention it to you earlier."

"She was in a hurry when she dropped me off."

"That woman is always in a hurry. Anyway, Carly wanted me to ask if you'd go."

"I'm a little tired."

"I know. But it would mean a lot to her. Gabriel and I have friends all over England, but you're pretty much the only one who will be there for Carly."

"In that case, of course I'll go."

"Good. Now, here's the next thing. Carly has an appointment before the party. It has something to do with honeymoon plans she wants to surprise Gabriel with. I'm taking her, of course. If Gabriel did, there wouldn't be much of a surprise. Would you mind coming to the party with Gabriel? It'll save us a little time if we don't have to come back here to pick you up."

"If that's what she wants." Kate turned her head and looked in the direction Gabriel had disappeared. "Although I don't know how happy he'll be about it."

Richard flashed her his most charming smile. "If you don't find him to your taste, I'll be more than happy to take over the escort duties later in the evening. You see, Kate, it might take me a while, but I'll win you over eventually. You will like me."

Kate returned his smile with a "don't count on it" one of her own. "What time?"

"Eight o'clock, maybe a little later. Make sure you eat something before you go. It's not a dinner party."

"All right. And I'll try to find something to wear."

"Thanks."

The two of them fell into step as they walked toward the house. "Have you seen the gardens yet?" he asked.

"No. I went straight to the cliffs."

"Don't miss them. They're spectacular by anyone's standards. Even mine. Gabriel designed the landscaping at the same time he designed the house."

As they rounded the corner, Kate spotted her sister's car. "Good, she's back. I'm going to talk to her."

"Don't keep her too long. We have to leave soon. Remind her for me, will you?"

"Sure. See you later." Kate walked quickly ahead of him and into the house.

When she got to her sister's room, Kate first listened for movement and then knocked on the door.

"Come in!" called Carly, sounding hurried.

Kate opened the door and peeked inside. It looked as if a hurricane had blown through, leaving destruction in its wake. Clothes had been thrown everywhere. "What happened in here?" asked Kate as she gingerly stepped between the pieces of clothing scattered on the floor.

"I can't decide what to wear." Carly held up a short black dress. "What do you think?"

"It's lovely."

"But it's black. Do you really think I should wear black? Do prospective brides wear black?"

"I imagine they wear any color they wish."

She looked at it in the mirror and wrinkled her nose. "Definitely not black." Tossing it on the bed, she then picked up a pale pink dress with a short skirt and plunging V neckline in both front and back. "What about this?"

"It's wonderful with your coloring. And very sexy." Kate cleared a spot on a chair and sat down. "Maybe it would help if you were to tell me what look you're trying to create. Do you want to look innocent? Classy? Sexy? Innocent and sexy at the same time?"

"I just want to look drop-dead gorgeous."

"For Gabriel or Richard?"

Carly grinned at her. "Both."

"Do you think that's wise?"

"I don't know about wise, but it's fun. Richard has quite a crush on me."

"So I gathered."

"Oh, don't take that disapproving tone. There's nothing between us except a harmless flirtation."

"When a fiancé's brother is involved, it's never harmless, and always dangerous."

"Just drop it, okay, Kate? I'm a big girl and I know what I'm doing." She held up another dress and modeled it in front of the mirror. "Did Richard ask if you'd go to the party with Gabriel?"

"Yes."

"Will you?"

"Of course, if that's what you want. I don't have anything to wear, though."

"Help yourself to whatever you need. I have more clothes than I'll ever wear. And there are some shopping bags in my closet with lingerie, jeans, sweaters, stuff like that. They were given to me after a photo shoot and I haven't worn them yet. I probably never will. They aren't really my taste. You can have those."

"Thanks."

Carly walked over the clothes on the floor in her stockinged feet to stand, hands on hips, in front of her closet. "I hate going to parties in the country."

"Why?"

"They're boring. I can't stand the people who live around here. You've never met such a bunch of stuffed shirts. You'll see what I mean tonight."

"Then why are you going?"

"Because they're Gabriel's friends and it's expected of me." She triumphantly pulled a white dress out of the closet and held it in front of her. "Ta-da. This should shake things up a little." Carly stood in front of the mirror and swayed back and forth. "Yeah. This is definitely the dress."

She unselfconsciously stripped out of everything but her panty hose and maneuvered herself into the second skin of a dress. "Zip me up, dear sister," she said as she leaned over her makeup table to touch up her lipstick.

Kate carefully picked her way back across the clothes and did as she was asked.

"Thanks." Carly tossed her lipstick down with a clatter, walked quickly back to her closet and emerged with a pair of very high, very white high heels. She leaned on Kate as she slipped on first one and then the other. "There. What do you think?" she asked as she straightened and stepped back so Kate could get a good look at her.

She thought Carly looked like a hooker, but magazines were full of models and actresses wearing exactly what Carly was. She'd no doubt paid a fortune for the dress—what there was of it.

"Well?"

"You look very fashionable," said Kate truthfully.

Carly turned to her mirror and smiled at herself. "I look incredible. Every man at the party is going to want me."

"Do you think perhaps you should try for a slightly more conservative appearance?"

"Then I'll look like everyone else. I want to stand out."

"You've definitely achieved that."

Carly gave her face a critical once-over, picked up a long-handled brush and added a touch more color to her cheeks. "You don't mind my turning you over to Gabriel for a few hours, do you?"

"Of course not. But he might."

"Why do you say that?"

"I saw him by the cliffs a little while ago. He was something less than friendly."

"Don't worry about that. He was probably preoccupied with his work. He usually is." Carly's eyes met Kate's in the mirror. "The nice thing is that tonight will give the two of you a chance to get to know one another a little before the wedding. Do me a favor, though, and don't give him chapter and verse on your past."

"Excuse me?"

"He doesn't need to know about Jeff and the baby."

"What on earth makes you think I would discuss that aspect of my life with anyone, much less some man I barely know?"

"Don't be offended. I just don't want my reputation with my new family tainted by your past. You have to admit that out-of-wedlock babies aren't exactly the rage these days."

Kate's throat tightened with hurt and anger, but she didn't dignify her sister's remarks with a response. It was just Carly once more talking without thinking.

"Gotta go," said Carly cheerfully, apparently oblivious to the pain she'd caused. "I'll see you and Gabriel later." With a wave of her fingers, she was out the door.

Once on the other side, Carly paused. The tiniest of smiles curved her mouth. There were times with Kate when it was almost too easy. Carly knew all of the right buttons to push to get to her.

Kate sat where she was for several minutes after Carly had gone. No matter how old Kate got, Carly still had the ability to knock the wind right out of her.

But she wouldn't let her sister get to her this time. With a sigh, she looked around the room and assessed the damage. It went against her nature to leave a place looking like this. Bending over, she picked things up from the floor and draped them over her arm, then carried them to the closet and put them on hangers. She found the bags her sister had told her about, and set those aside. Then she went through the closet looking for something to wear that evening. After much searching, she found a deep black cocktail dress with long sleeves and a slightly scooped neck that was much more her own conservative taste than Carly's, and took that for the party along with a pair of black high heels.

That done, she left Carly's room, head down as she looked inside one of the bags.

"I thought you were leaving with Richard."

Startled, Kate looked up and into the eyes of Gabriel Trent. The memory of their earlier encounter was still fresh in her mind. "It's me again. Kate."

Gabriel's expression didn't change.

Kate's mouth curved into a tentative smile. "It's hard for me to believe that in a very short time I'm going to be related to the famous Gabriel Trent."

Gabriel continued to stare at her, through her.

Kate's smile faded. "What's wrong?"

"You look exactly like your sister."

Suddenly she understood what was bothering him. "I know that can be distracting when people first see us together. There is actually a small difference. I have a tiny, heart-shaped freckle on my left thigh. My mother used it to tell us apart when we were babies."

He didn't say anything, but kept looking at her with those incredible golden brown eyes of his.

"When you get to know us better, you'll find we have very different personalities. Then you'll easily be able to tell the one you love from the one you don't."

Gabriel was still silent.

Kate nervously cleared her throat. "You're not a very talkative man, are you?"

He looked at his watch. "Excuse me."

"Of course. I'll see you later."

He turned to look at her. "What?"

"When we leave for the party."

"You're going?"

"I understood from Richard and Carly that I was to get a ride with you to a neighbor's house. Apparently no one told you. I'm sorry."

Gabriel was silent for several seconds. "Be ready at eight-thirty. I'll meet you downstairs."

Before she could respond, Gabriel was gone.

Kate stood rooted to the spot as her eyes followed him. The man clearly didn't like her at all and she had no idea what she'd done to cause that kind of reaction.

The short time before the wedding was seeming longer all the time.

With a shake of her head, Kate turned and went to her room, where she showered and put on the black dress. It fit her like a glove, which meant that it must have been too big for Carly. The bodice was fitted, but began a gentle flare at about hip level, stopping eight inches above her knees. It was a simple style that suited her figure. If she hadn't known better, she would have thought that Carly had bought it with her in mind.

She brushed her auburn hair in long strokes, deciding to leave it down since Carly was wearing hers up.

Leaning toward the mirror, Kate gave herself a critical once-over. She only had lipstick and powder to work with since the rest of her makeup was with her luggage. She could have borrowed some of Carly's, but somehow what she had on seemed to be enough.

Her stomach rumbled.

Dinner. She needed some food and decided to take Richard's advice about having dinner before going to the party. She still had more than an hour to wait.

Going downstairs, she paused in the foyer, not sure which way to go. A little girl of perhaps five or six with auburn hair and wide blue eyes skipped past her.

"Wait!" called Kate with a smile.

The little girl stopped and turned, but didn't smile and made no move toward her.

Kate covered the distance between them, her hand extended. "Hi. My name is Kate."

The little girl frowned, clearly confused.

Kate knelt so that they were eye level. "You know my name. May I know yours?"

The little girl still looked suspicious, but she politely extended her small hand.

"Are you Willa?"

"You know I am. And you're not Kate. You're Carly."

"I'm Carly's twin sister."

"Oh!" Suspicion was replaced with a smile. "I have some friends who are twins. They look the same, too. I think it's weird to have someone look just like you."

"There are times when I think it's weird, too," Kate agreed.

Willa was a beautiful child. Her waist-length auburn hair was held away from her face by a dark velvet headband. A strand had come loose and Kate reached up and tucked it behind her ear in a gesture that came naturally. "How old are you?"

"Six." She said it with a hint of a lisp.

"Do you go to school?"

"Of course."

Kate smiled. "Silly question. Sorry." Kate stood up.

"I'm going to see my nana. Would you like to come with me?"

"I'd like that very much, thank you."

Willa trustingly took her hand and led Kate down a series of spacious hallways that would themselves have qualified as rooms, right down to the occasional intimate furniture groupings that lent themselves to cozy conversation. Off one of the hallways were ten-foot-high double doors that opened into a salon.

As Kate passed through the doors, she stopped to look around. It was a glorious combination of old-fashioned and modern. A shiny black grand piano with its lid propped open sat between two floor-to-ceiling windows. Cozy natural white couches and overstuffed chairs were grouped near a marble fireplace where the flames burned low, taking the chill out of the evening air. The soft sounds of Mozart hung in the room, lending an almost enchanted feeling.

An older woman with curling white hair was sitting in a high-backed, tapestry-covered chair, her half glasses on the end of her nose, doing needlepoint. She looked over the tops of her glasses at Willa and Kate.

Willa dropped Kate's hand and leaned against the woman's chair. "This is Nana," she announced.

The woman put her arm around Willa and hugged her. "Dear, Carly knows who I am."

Kate stepped forward, her hand extended. "I'm so sorry to spring myself on you like this. I'm Carly's sister, Kate. It seems no one was expecting me but Carly."

The older woman, clearly surprised, took Kate's hand in hers and held it for a moment while she looked into Kate's eyes. Like Willa, she seemed suspicious. "I'm Laurel Trent, this little one's great-grandmother. I wasn't aware that we had company."

"I'm really sorry, Mrs. Trent. I hope it's not inconvenient."

"You're welcome here, of course." She released Kate's hand. "Please, have a seat."

"Thank you."

"Do you have plans for the evening?" she asked, looking at the way Kate was dressed.

"Yes. Apparently I'm going to some kind of party at a neighbor's home. I don't know any other details."

The older woman nodded. "The Granvilles. I'd forgotten that was this evening."

"Carly and Richard have left already. I'm supposed to follow later with Gabriel."

"If you're going to be here for a while, would you care to join Willa and me for dinner?"

"I'd love to," said Kate. "In fact, I was looking for food when I ran into Willa."

"Good." She turned to her great-granddaughter. "Willa, tell Cook that there will be three of us for dinner."

"Yes, ma'am."

"What about Gabriel?"

"He's working. I'm sure he'll eat something later." Both women watched Willa as she skipped out of the room.

"She's a beautiful child." Kate had no idea how wistful her voice sounded.

Laurel Trent studied Kate's expression to see if there was anything behind the words. "Yes, she is. And a good child, as well. Gabriel has been a wonderful father to her."

Kate felt the words were, for some reason, aimed at her.

"I don't know what he'd do if anything ever happened to her."

Kate nodded. "A parent's worst nightmare."

Again the older woman studied the younger. "It was just a figure of speech, dear." She made a stitch, then held the canvas up to the light to look at it. "I'm just not sure about the color."

Kate left her chair to look at it herself. It was an Oriental design, remarkably detailed and a very complicated piece of work. "This is beautiful."

The older woman nodded. "I agree. What do you think about this gold?" She pointed the needle at a small square of stitches.

Kate studied it for a few moments. "I think a brighter yellow would be better. It needs more contrast." She pointed to another area that was destined for the same gold. "Over here, too. It's more vivid."

She nodded. "I see what you're saying. Do you do needlepoint yourself?"

"I did when I was in college. It relaxed me—particularly during exams."

"And now?"

"I tend to read in my spare time. Work consumes most of my days."

"You young people need to take more time for yourselves. I'm constantly telling Gabriel that." She watched Kate retake her seat. "Are you married?"

"No."

"Not ever or just not now?"

Kate smiled. "Not ever."

"Did you come close?"

"Just once," said Kate without explanation.

"What happened? Did you come to your senses?"
Her smile faded. "He died."

"Oh, I'm so sorry. Leave it to me to walk into something like that with a flip remark."

Kate liked this woman.

"What about Carly?"

"Carly?"

"We haven't had much of a chance to get to know one another. I confess I'm curious about her. Has she been married before?"

"No. As a matter of fact, I don't think she's ever really been in love until now."

"I see." She finished a stitch and looked at Kate over the top of her half glasses. "I imagine the two of you are close."

"Not as close as I'd like. Sometimes we go for months without talking or seeing one another."

"What about your parents?"

"Our father left home when we were young. I understand that he died a few years ago."

"And your mother?"

"She's still living in Chicago."

"I look forward to meeting her when she arrives for the wedding. That will be soon, I imagine."

Kate looked as uneasy as she felt. "Our mother probably won't be coming."

"Good heavens, why not?"

"She's very busy."

Laurel glanced at Kate and went back to her stitching. "How odd. I can't think of anything that would have kept me away from my daughter's wedding."

"This all came up rather suddenly. It's difficult for her to get away on such short notice." She inwardly apologized for coloring the truth. "I know it's the bride's family that traditionally hosts the wedding. I want you to know that I'll do whatever I can to help."

"Thank you, dear. Because of the timing, it's being thrown together rather quickly. Gabriel, of course, is no help at all. The less fuss, the happier he is."

Willa skipped back into the room, "I told Mrs. Meredith. She's setting an extra place."

"Thank you, sweetheart."

Willa smiled as she leaned on the arm of her great-grandmother's chair. "When Carly marries my dad, what will that make you to me?"

Kate had to think for a moment. "I believe I'll be your step-aunt."

"So I should call you Aunt Kate?"

"If you'd like. I think that would be lovely," said Kate.

"But I can't do that until you're really my aunt."

"You can just call me Kate in the meantime."

"I'm afraid I don't approve of children calling adults by their first names," Mrs. Trent interrupted. "This is certainly a different world from the one I grew up in."

Again she watched Kate, searching her face for any clue that she knew Willa's true relationship to her. But Kate was far too natural around the child to be harboring any dark secrets. Either that or she was quite an actress.

A heavy older woman came into the room. "Excuse me, madam," she said in a thick Scots accent, "but the meal is ready."

"Thank you, Mrs. Meredith. You're free to go home now if you wish."

She inclined her head.

"Oh! Before you go, I'd like you to meet Carly's twin sister, Kate."

The cook looked surprised as she nodded her head.

Kate smiled at her. "How do you do?"

"It's nice to meet you," Mrs. Meredith said, discreetly withdrawing from the room.

Putting aside her needlepoint, Laurel Trent rose from the chair with the grace of a much younger woman. "Come, ladies."

She led the way to a cozy formal dining room. The round table was set with fine china and candles. Several covered dishes sat elegantly on the sideboard.

They started with a lovely cream of asparagus soup that was in a small tureen. Kate ladled some into Willa's bowl first, then into her own, and joined Gabriel's grandmother at the table.

"How long have you lived here?" said Kate.

"Nearly six years. I came here from Boston to help Gabriel raise Willa when his wife died."

Willa kept an eye on Kate while they ate, smiling whenever Kate looked at her.

Kate winked at her. Willa's version of winking back was to scrunch both eyes tightly closed and then open them wide.

"How did your grandson come to live in England?" asked Kate.

"I myself was married to an Englishman, and our son in turn married an Englishwoman. Gabriel and Richard were both born in London and, for the most part, have spent their lives in one part of England or another."

"Was Gabriel's first wife English?"

"Yes, she was. Would you be a dear and get me a dinner roll from the sideboard?"

"Of course." Kate picked up the basket of rolls and handed them to her before retaking her seat.

Willa wrinkled her nose at Kate.

Kate wrinkled right back at her.

Mrs. Trent discreetly watched the two of them and smiled to herself.

Dinner continued pleasantly, and soon they moved on to dessert.

"Willa, I want you to take your bath as soon as we've finished eating and get yourself ready for bed."

"Yes, ma'am." She looked hopefully at Kate. "Will you read me my bedtime story tonight since my dad is working?"

"Of course. I'd love to."

The little girl smiled as she dug into her dessert.

Kate was too full to eat dessert, but sat back and enjoyed watching Willa. Willa kept glancing up at her, a mischievous twinkle in her pretty blue eyes.

After a few minutes, her spoon clattered onto her plate. "May I please be excused now, Nana?"

"Of course, dear. Start your bath and I'll be up shortly."

"Can Kate come instead?"

"That's entirely up to her."

Two pairs of eyes swung in Kate's direction. "I'm yours to command," she told the child with a smile.

"Then I command you."

"So be it."

Willa ran to her great-grandmother and hugged her. "Love you. Good night."

"Sweet dreams."

Kate watched with warmly smiling eyes as the child rushed out of the room. "I don't think I've ever seen a six-year-old in such a hurry to take a bath."

"Don't be fooled. It isn't the bath. It's the story. She loves being read to."

"Does she read herself yet?"

"Oh, yes. Quite well, in fact. But as you might remember from your own childhood, there's nothing quite like being read to. I still enjoy it myself from time to time." She leaned back in her chair and eyed Kate. "Willa is quite taken with you."

"That's because I'm so much like Carly."

Mrs. Trent cleared her throat as she placed her napkin neatly on the table. "Yes, well, I rather think you've won her over on your own merits."

"I hope so. She's a lovely little girl." Kate looked at her watch. "It's been a few minutes. Should I go to Willa now?"

"Yes, I suppose so. Her room is on the second floor to the left of the staircase, fourth door down."

"Thank you."

"As for me," she said as she rose, "I think I'll retire early tonight. I feel a little headache coming on."

"Can I get you something?"

"No, thank you, dear. A good night's rest and I'll be as good as new in the morning."

"Sleep well."

The older woman watched as Kate left the room. Interesting. She had very little use for Carly, but Kate was another matter entirely. She was a lovely young woman and, despite her resemblance to Carly, Mrs. Trent found herself quite liking Kate.

Chapter Three

When Kate arrived upstairs, Willa was already in her flowered nightgown, sitting on the floor in front of her bookcase. Kate stood in the doorway and watched her with a wistful smile that touched her eyes. She could have looked at Willa forever.

"Did you finish your bath already?" asked Kate as she crossed the room and sat on the floor next to the child.

"Yes."

"You're very grown-up for a six-year-old. I don't think my mother let me take baths on my own until I was eight. Maybe nine."

"I don't have a mother," Willa said matter-of-factly. "She died."

"I know. I'm sorry. You must miss her very much."
Willa nodded.

"But soon you'll have Carly to help you with things."

Willa's shoulders suddenly straightened. Kate recognized the body language.

"Of course, no one will ever be able to take your mother's place, and I'm sure Carly won't try to do that. You'll just have to let her know what you want her to do and what you don't want her to do."

"I guess," said Willa with a shrug as she pulled a book off the shelf. "Do you like Dr. Seuss?"

Kate followed Willa's lead and dropped her questioning. "He's one of my favorites."

"Which book do you like best?"

Kate thought for a moment. "Well, it's a toss-up between *Horton Hatches an Egg* and *Horton Hears a Who.*"

Willa beamed as she showed Kate the book she'd chosen. "I like Horton, too." She rose, bounded across the room and jumped on her bed. "I'm ready."

"Did you brush your teeth?" asked Kate as she rose from the floor.

"Yes."

"And your hair?"

"My hair?"

Kate picked up a brush from the dresser and walked to the bed. "May I?"

"Sure." Willa turned to sit sideways, and Kate sat behind her, brushing her coppery hair in long strokes.

"When I was small, my mother would brush my hair a hundred strokes every night," said Kate.

"Why?"

"She said it was the only way to have really beautiful hair."

"Is that true?"

"I don't know, but to this day, I still do it every night."

Willa looked over her shoulder at Kate. "And you have beautiful hair, so it must be true."

Kate impulsively kissed the top of her head. "Face forward. You're making me lose count."

As she gently pulled the brush through the child's silky hair, Kate tried hard to swallow the lump in her throat. Her own daughter, had she lived past the day of her birth, would have been about the same age as Willa. She would have brushed her own child's hair just the way she was brushing Willa's.

"Do you have any children?" asked Willa innocently.

It was a moment before Kate trusted herself to answer in a normal voice. "No."

"Do you want to?"

"Someday. Do you?"

Willa laughed. "That's a silly question. I'm only six."

"What about when you're older?"

"I think having lots of children would be fun. A whole houseful of them. That way they'll always have someone to play with. Are you almost finished?"

"Ninety-eight, ninety-nine, one hundred. All done."
Kate slid off the bed and put the brush on the dresser.

Walking back to the bed, she stacked some pillows against the headboard and leaned against them. "Now for the story."

Willa cuddled up beside her and Kate put an arm around her. "Comfortable?"

Willa nodded against her shoulder.

As Kate opened to the first, familiar page, she said, "I should warn you, I do all of the voices."

Willa smiled and waited expectantly.

Kate couldn't have asked for a better audience. Willa loved Kate's rendition of Horton's voice and lowered her chin to her chest when she tried to imitate the low-voiced lisp Kate gave the character. And Willa flew into gales of laughter when she heard Maizie Bird's nasal whine.

As soon as they'd finished that story, Willa handed her the other Horton book and looked at her expectantly.

Kate looked at her watch. She still had half an hour before she had to leave. "This is the last one. Then it's lights-out, all right?"

Willa nodded and snuggled against her again.

And so Kate launched into another round of voices.

When she finished the last page, Willa settled under her covers while Kate climbed off the bed, laid the book on the end table and rearranged the pillows so Willa would be more comfortable. "How's that?"

"Fine, thank you. Will you read to me again to-morrow night?"

"If you'd like me to, of course."

Willa smiled as she wrapped her arms around Kate's neck and hugged her tightly.

Kate was so startled that at first she just stood there. But then her arms automatically went around Willa and hugged her back. "Good night, sweetheart."

"Are you going to sleep now, too?"

"No. I have to go somewhere with your father in a few minutes."

She pulled the covers up a little higher, leaned over and kissed Willa's childishly rounded cheek. "Good night," she said softly. Straightening, she reached for the light.

"Don't!" said Willa. "I like the light on."

"This one's too bright to leave on." Kate looked around the room and spotted a lamp on the dresser. "How about that one?"

"All right."

So Kate turned off the light by the bed and turned on the one on the dresser. As she made her way to the door, Willa's childish voice stopped her again.

"I can't sleep."

Kate turned with twinkling eyes. "I think you need to give it a little more time."

"I can't sleep. Please don't go."

"But..."

"Please?"

Kate couldn't say no to that sweet little plea. "All right," she said as she closed the door and came back to the bed. "I'll stay for a few more minutes."

"Here." Willa patted the covers beside her.

Kate lay on top of them, her head on the pillows. Willa maneuvered herself under Kate's arm and let out a long, contented sigh.

Kate lay there for the longest time listening to Willa's short and soft breaths. She couldn't remember the last time she'd felt so completely at peace. It wasn't just that Willa was a child. Kate had been around many children since she lost her own. It was Willa herself. She touched something deep inside Kate that had been safely locked away for more than six years.

It's getting late, thought Kate as she drifted into sleep, her arm still around Willa, her cheek resting on top of the little girl's head.

Gabriel, dressed in a tuxedo, left his room and walked down the hall to say good-night to his daughter. Carefully opening the door so it wouldn't make any noise, he walked into her bedroom and stopped short. For a moment, he thought it was Carly lying there. Then he realized it couldn't be. It had to be Kate.

He moved closer and looked at the two of them, sleeping so innocently, their faces close together.

For the first time, he realized just how much alike they looked. Even Kate's hair was just a darker version of Willa's. His eyes moved over Kate's face feature by feature.

As though she was aware of being watched, Kate opened her eyes and looked directly at Gabriel. Her mouth curved into a warm, sleepy smile that made Gabriel's heart catch unexpectedly. His expression hardened.

Kate's smile faltered as Gabriel gestured toward the door.

Wondering what she'd done wrong, she carefully took her arm from around Willa and rose from the bed.

Gabriel leaned over his daughter, looked at her for a long moment and kissed her forehead, then put his hand in the middle of Kate's back and firmly guided her from the room, leaving the door open a crack.

"I'm sorry," Kate whispered. "I didn't mean to fall asleep. I'll just brush my hair and then I'll be ready to go."

"What were you doing there in the first place?" His voice was quiet, but his tone was clearly hostile.

Kate looked at him in surprise. "Willa asked me to read a story to her."

Gabriel stopped walking and turned to face Kate. "Stay away from my daughter."

"What?" She looked as bewildered as she felt.

"Stay away from her." Though he still spoke quietly, there was no mistaking the force behind his words. As he started to walk past her, Kate caught his arm.

"You can't just give an order like that and walk away without any explanation."

"Yes, I can."

"I want to know why and I deserve an answer."

"Willa is my child, and I decide who spends time with her—and who doesn't."

"That's it?"

"In a nutshell."

"Well, that's no reason at all. It's just a pronouncement."

His eyes burned through her. "Look, Ms. Fairfax, I don't owe you an explanation for anything I do. Just keep away from my daughter."

"I see."

"I hope so."

"You should talk to your grandmother about this. She encouraged me to read to Willa tonight." Gabriel heard the anger in her voice. "And I'll tell you something else. Willa enjoyed my company every bit as much as I enjoyed hers. By punishing me, you're punishing her. Is that your intention?"

"My intention is to protect my child."

"From me?" Kate asked in astonishment. "You want to protect her from me? What have I ever done to you?"

Gabriel was silent.

Kate tiredly rubbed her forehead and let out a long breath. "Look," she said more calmly, "you've had a problem with me since I arrived. I don't know what I've done to offend you, so I don't know how to fix it. I guess the good news for you is that I'll be gone after the wedding and then neither of us will have to deal with each other any longer."

A door across the hall opened, framing a pink-robed Laurel Trent. "What are you two going on about?"

He continued to stare at Kate. "I'm sorry, Grandmother. I didn't mean to disturb you."

"Well, you did. What time is it?"

Gabriel looked at his watch. "Ten o'clock."

"I thought the two of you were supposed to go to a party. What are you still doing here?"

"I was working and lost track of the time."

"But the Granvilles are expecting both of you. This is very rude."

"Grandmother . . ."

"Kate, you're mussed. Go to your room and freshen up. Gabriel, I'd like to speak with you."

As quickly as that, Kate's mood changed from anger to amusement, and her eyes sparkled. It was refreshing to hear Gabriel being spoken to as though he were a child.

Gabriel, however, was most definitely not amused. His eyes narrowed.

Kate sucked in her cheeks to hide her smile, but Gabriel saw it anyway. "I'll be right back," she said brightly.

"Meet me downstairs," said Gabriel.

Kate let herself smile all she wanted as she walked away, unaware of Gabriel's eyes on her. When she got to her room, she leaned against her door. It was amazing how a dressing-down from a grandmother could take a man down a few pegs. What kind of man would talk back to his own grandmother?

Laurel Trent studied her grandson as he watched Kate. "She's a lovely young woman, isn't she?"

"She's Carly's sister."

"I like her."

"You don't know her."

"And you do?"

"I know her twin. That's as close as I want to get."

"She's not like Carly. I can tell by looking into her eyes."

"Grandmother..."

"It's true. Carly's eyes are kind of dead. Kate's sparkle with life."

"You can't tell anything about a person from looking into their eyes. The fact is, the woman's a Fairfax. As such, she's a threat to Willa. I don't want anyone from that family left alone with my daughter."

"It was what Willa wanted."

"Grandmother, you know what's going on here. You can't trust either of those women."

Laurel moved aside and waved him into her room. "Come in here."

Gabriel stepped into a sitting room, where a table lamp offered its golden glow.

"I don't want Willa to accidentally hear any of this. You must know," she said as she closed the door, "that if I thought for a moment that Kate was a threat to Willa's safety, I wouldn't have let her anywhere near the child."

Gabriel dragged his fingers tiredly through his hair. "I don't know anything anymore."

Laurel's heart ached for her grandson. He was a good man and he didn't deserve what was happening to him. "I'm sorry, Gabriel. I know this is difficult for you. But for what it's worth, I don't think Kate knows what's going on."

"Of course she does."

"No," said Laurel with a shake of her head. "I watched her closely all evening. I really don't think she knows that Willa is her sister's daughter. And I also don't think she has any idea that Carly's blackmailing you into marriage."

"And you've based these conclusions on . . . ?"

"Kate's nature."

"Let me guess," he asked with a wry smile. "You know all about her nature because of her eyes."

"Exactly. If that girl had any idea about what Carly's doing to you, I don't believe she would have come here at all. She wouldn't have been able to face us."

He kissed her forehead. "You always see the best in everyone. That's one of the many reasons I love you. This time, though, I think you're seeing qualities that aren't there."

"What do you see when you look at her?"

"A mirror image of a woman I loathe."

"They're separate people, Gabriel."

"Maybe. But I can't look at one without seeing the other."

His grandmother got a faraway look in her eyes.

"What is it?"

"I didn't think about it until I saw Kate with Willa, but it strikes me as odd that Carly claims to want her daughter to the point where she threatens to take her away from you, and yet since arriving here, she's hardly spent any time with the child at all."

"And your conclusion?"

"I don't think Carly is interested in Willa at all, as a mother or anything else."

"She must be, or I wouldn't be marrying her."

"I think there's something else going on."

"If you figure it out, let me know."

"You might be closer to the answer than you think."

"What do you mean?"

"Kate."

"I thought you don't believe she knows anything."

"And I stand by that. But that doesn't mean she won't find out—and maybe soon enough to prevent the wedding."

"Why would she betray her sister to help me?"

"I'm sure she won't, considering the way you've been treating her. Think about it. She's the one person who might be able to help you out of this, and you've been alienating her every step of the way."

"You're wrong. If the woman is as honorable as you seem to think, there's no way she'll turn on her sister."

"I've seen the way she reacts to Willa. If she gets close to the child and comes to believe that her sister means to harm her, I believe the child is the one she'll try to protect, not Carly."

"Why should Kate care about what happens to Willa?"

"I can't explain it, but she does. There's a connection between the two of them, and you'd do well to foster that instead of trying to keep them apart."

"I won't use my daughter."

"She's my great-granddaughter, and I love her every bit as much as you do. I'm not saying you should encourage Willa to have a relationship with Kate. I'm just saying that you shouldn't intrude on what's happening naturally. Kate could turn out to be the saving grace of this family. But not if you continue to treat her like the enemy." She looked at the clock on the mantel over her fireplace. "You should leave. Kate's probably waiting for you."

He rose from his chair, leaned over and kissed his grandmother on top of her head. "Get some sleep. I'll talk to you in the morning."

She watched him leave with worried eyes. She had helped raise him the same way she was helping to raise Willa. Gabriel the child and now the man kept his feelings to himself, his emotions buried. But she knew just how angry he was at Carly for the threat she posed.

Kate brushed her hair, touched up her makeup and hurried downstairs and out the front door.

Gabriel, leaning against the passenger door of the car, his arms folded across his chest, watched as she walked toward him. There was a momentary hesitation in her movement when she saw him.

He noticed.

While in her room, Kate had decided that she quite simply wasn't going to argue with the man. He was going to marry her sister and she was going to get along with him if it killed her. He looked as though he'd just showered and shaved, but there was a hint of dark shadow on his cheeks. His long, wavy hair was still damp. A thin scar ran the length of his cheek. His jaw was strong with a hint of a crease in his chin. And his lips looked as though they'd been etched by an artist. *Chiseled* was a word that came to mind.

He was the kind of man it was hard to look away from. Not just because he was so handsome, but also because he had a presence that demanded acknowledgment. This was the kind of man who could capture the attention of a roomful of people by simply walking through the door.

Carly was a lucky woman. And she would most certainly never be bored.

"I'm sorry I took so long," Kate said as she stopped in front of Gabriel. "I had to do more damage control than I anticipated."

His eyes moved over her face. "Nice job."

"Thanks." She smiled at him. If all else failed, she'd charm him into liking her.

"Don't worry about the time. We're already two hours late. A few more minutes won't make any difference." He opened the door and waited for Kate to get settled. Leaning over her, he snapped her seat belt into place. Kate, caught off guard by his nearness, pressed herself back into the seat as far as she could until he straightened away from her. He smelled wonderful. "Thank you."

"Yeah," he said as he closed her door.

Kate watched him walk around the front of the car and climb into the driver's side. He was absolutely silent as he pulled the car away from the house, but she had the distinct feeling that he was less hostile and she responded accordingly.

Kate had a hundred questions. "Carly hasn't told me much about you. I know you're an architect because I'm an admirer of your work."

He didn't say anything.

"I think it's wonderful how the two of you met and knew instantly that you were in love. That doesn't happen very often."

Gabriel glanced at her, then looked back at the road. "I'm not interested in having this conversation with you."

"Okay," said Kate, undaunted. "What kind of conversation are you interested in?"

"Silence is a pleasant option."

"You don't do small talk?"

"Not if I can help it."

Kate sighed. "Why exactly don't you like me?"

"You sound as though it's a new experience for you."

"I'm sure I've met people over the years who haven't liked me. They've just been more circumspect about it."

"Do you prefer the more direct approach or the less obvious one?"

"It's a tough call. On the one hand, it's nice to know where you stand with a person. On the other hand, the truth hurts."

A corner of his mouth lifted, deepening the groove in his cheek.

One point for her. "You're different from the men my sister is usually attracted to."

"In what way?"

"Less charming. More mysterious. More interesting."

"Are you saying that you find rude and enigmatic men more appealing?"

"Than what?"

"Polite and like a book you've already read."

"In my own life, I've leaned more toward the polite, used-book sort."

"Why?"

"They're usually much safer."

"Is safety important to you?"

"Very."

"What do you think that means?"

"I've actually given this some thought, and I decided it means that I crave stability."

"Did you have a tumultuous childhood?"

Kate lifted her shoulders in a delicate shrug. "I had the same childhood Carly had." She studied his profile. "For someone who likes silence, you ask a lot of questions."

"At the moment, I find you more interesting than silence."

"Thank you—I think."

A minute later, Gabriel turned the car down a semicircular driveway and parked behind a long line of cars that stretched its length. Kate didn't wait for him to open her door, but stepped out on her own. Gabriel came around the car and put his hand politely under her elbow as they walked toward the large, modern home.

Kate was busy looking at the well-lit lawn when her high heel caught on a crack in the sidewalk. When she pitched forward, Gabriel caught her with his hands at her waist. Kate looked up at him with a smile. "Nice save. Thanks."

"You're welcome."

The music grew louder the closer they drew to the open double doors. There was a steady, low hum of conversation punctuated by laughter. As they walked through the main hall with its elegant mosaic tiles, Gabriel said hello to some people standing in a group talking. He didn't introduce Kate, but that was all right with her. She was really too tired to make a lot of small talk.

Walking ahead of him, Kate made her way to the source of most of the noise and stood in the doorway looking around. People were dancing to a live band that was playing at the far end of one of the largest single rooms Kate had ever seen. It looked as though it had been designed specifically for parties like this.

She knew without having to see when Gabriel came up behind her. She looked over her shoulder and smiled at him.

He frowned in return.

Kate turned completely around to face him. With a gentle finger, she smoothed the frown line on his forehead. "And you were doing so well," she said regretfully. "I was almost looking forward to having you in the family."

Gabriel had to admit that he was charmed in spite of himself. He caught her hand in his and held it. "Dance with me."

Kate couldn't have been more surprised. "Really?"

"Really."

"I'd like that."

Still holding her hand, he led her onto the dance floor, then stopped and turned to her. Keeping some distance between them, he put one hand at her waist and held her hand in his other. Kate let her left hand rest on his shoulder. Steering her gently but firmly, he moved her around the floor with a skill she hadn't expected from such a tall man.

"You're good," she said, smiling up at him.

"So are you."

"My well-intentioned mother forced me to take ballroom dancing when I was ten."

Gabriel nodded knowingly. "Boys lined up at one end of the room and girls at the other?"

She nodded. "White gloves."

"Tie and jacket."

"It sounds as though you went through the same torture."

"You've met my grandmother," he said dryly.

"She's a wonderful woman."

"Yes. I don't know what Willa and I would have done without her after my wife died."

"That must have been a terrible time for you."

"It was. I still miss her." Gabriel couldn't believe he was talking to her about Stephanie. He never talked to anyone about her. Not even his grandmother.

Another couple bumped into them and pushed Kate into Gabriel. She looked up at him full of apology. "I'm sorry."

Gabriel didn't even realize he'd stopped dancing as he looked at Kate, her face close to his. He moved his hand from her waist to her back and began swaying in rhythm with the music. Kate moved with him, suddenly very aware of her body: her breasts pressed against his chest; her thighs rubbed his with every movement; her cheek brushed against the material of his jacket and she breathed in the scent of his skin. She was shocked by her body's response.

Kate suddenly stopped dancing and stepped back.

Gabriel didn't ask her what was wrong.

He knew.

He'd felt it, too.

Chapter Four

"There you are!" called out Carly as she made her way toward them.

Kate and Gabriel continued to stare at each other.

Carly looped her arm through Gabriel's. "Did you just get here?"

It was Kate who dragged her eyes from Gabriel and tried to focus on her sister. "A few minutes ago."

"I was beginning to think you weren't coming at all." She waved at Richard, who had come up behind Kate. "You dance with my sister." Then she moved herself into Gabriel's seemingly reluctant arms. "And you, my love, dance with me."

Richard tapped Kate on the shoulder. She turned and forced a smile to her lips. "Hello."

He opened his arms into a dance pose, "Shall we?"

Kate put her hand in his and off they went, swaying gracefully among the other couples. "Did your grandmother make you take ballroom dancing, too?"

"Oh," he groaned, "don't remind me."

"Did you and Gabriel go together?"

"No. I'm five years younger than he is."

"I didn't know."

"No reason you should."

"Do you live with Gabriel or are you visiting?"

"Let's just say that I've been visiting him for the past six months."

Kate smiled. "I see."

"My inheritance is running a little low. I need time to regroup before going back out into the cold, cruel world."

"Don't you work?"

"No. I never figured out what it was I wanted to do with my life."

"So you're doing nothing?"

"Exactly."

"Doesn't that bother you?"

"Not at all. Pathetic, aren't I?"

Kate couldn't help laughing.

Gabriel watched Kate dancing with his brother. He saw her laugh. His grandmother was right about her eyes.

"We need to talk," said Carly.

Gabriel reluctantly looked at the woman he was going to marry. "About what?"

"My sister. I don't want her to know about Willa. And I don't want her to know why you're marrying me."

"Why not? What difference could it possibly make?"

"This is between you and me. It doesn't have anything to do with her. She doesn't even know I had a child six years ago."

"You're kidding."

"I'm not. And I won't have her finding out now unless and until I decide to tell her."

"And if she finds out by accident?"

Carly looked at him with a steady gaze. "Then I'll make a call to my attorney and you can expect to lose Willa. And I'll tell you something else. You'd better treat me the way a man is supposed to treat the woman he intends to marry, especially in public. I won't be humiliated in front of these people or my own family."

"I'm an architect, not an actor."

"Just do the best you can. It's important to me that Kate thinks we're in love."

The muscle in Gabriel's jaw tightened. "Why are you doing this? What's the point in blackmailing your way into a loveless marriage with a man who loathes the sight of you? What do you gain?"

"A husband, a daughter, respectability and some things you couldn't begin to understand."

"I'll never love you."

"But Kate doesn't know that."

"What does she have to do with any of this?"

Carly looked at him for a long moment. "Just don't tell her. If you do, you'll pay."

The song came to an end and the small orchestra announced that they were going to take a break. Gabriel's arms fell instantly to his sides. He couldn't stand touching her.

Carly ignored the message behind his gesture and put her arm through his as she steered him toward the bar. "Let's get a drink, darling."

At the same time, Richard was leading Kate through the other couples on the dance floor and toward the bar. They arrived at almost the same moment as Carly and Gabriel.

Kate barely glanced at Gabriel. Her body still hadn't settled down from their dance.

"What would you like?" asked Richard.

"I don't know. A soda, I guess."

"Nothing harder?"

"I'm so tired that one drink would do me in."

"Gotcha." He asked for her soda and a Scotch on the rocks for himself.

Carly, still possessively hanging on to Gabriel, smiled at her sister. "I'm sorry I wasn't able to spend more time with you today."

"That's all right. I know you're busy. How did the fitting go?"

"The dress is stunning, Kate. Wait till you see it. It was designed especially for me."

"I know you'll be a beautiful bride."

"Don't be jealous, though. Someday you'll find the man who's just right for you."

Kate smiled at her sister. "I'm happy for you, Carly, not jealous. And I'm not going to hold my breath waiting for Mr. Right."

Carly nodded. "Of course. You already found him once, didn't you?"

Kate's smile faded.

"Sorry. I didn't mean to bring up painful memories." She let go of Gabriel's arm and hugged Kate. "I wasn't thinking."

Gabriel watched the two of them. He knew what kind of woman Carly was. It wasn't clear to him that Kate did, however.

"Here you go," said Richard as he handed her a soda.

"Thank you." Kate took a long sip as she looked around the room—anywhere but at Gabriel. Finally her gaze rested on Richard. "This is a lovely party."

"The Granvilles always give nice parties. I'll introduce you as soon as I spot one of them."

"Are they close friends of yours?"

"They're Gabriel's friends more than mine."

Carly waved to someone across the room. "Excuse me, Katie. I see someone I need to talk to." She went up on her toes and kissed Gabriel on the cheek. "Don't be too lonely without me."

Gabriel was as unresponsive as Kate had ever seen a man.

Richard, on the other hand, did everything but drool as he watched Carly walk away. Kate lightly smacked his arm with the back of her hand. "You shouldn't be looking at her like that."

"Women can't wear dresses that fit the way that one does and expect men not to look. The whole purpose of wearing an outfit like that is to get men to look."

Kate dared to glance at Gabriel. He wasn't paying any attention to Carly at all, which she found curious.

His eyes met Kate's for a long moment, and then he turned and walked away.

"What's your brother's story?"

"What do you mean?"

"Most people you meet are easy to figure out. He's not."

"That's true. I'm his brother and I have no idea where he's coming from."

"You sound as though you don't like him very much."

Richard took a long swig of his Scotch. "I respect him. I admire him. But Gabriel isn't what I consider a very likable man."

"That's blunt."

"You're right. Too blunt. Let's just say that Gabriel isn't the kind of man I'd choose to have as a friend. He isn't my idea of buddy material. He never does anything that's fun. Everything in his life is responsibility. He reeks of it."

"Which, of course, goes against everything you believe in."

"You got that right." He said hello to a woman who walked past them. "Don't misunderstand me. I might not like the guy, but I love him. There's no one in the world I trust more than Gabriel." He stared into his drink.

"So what's the real problem?" asked Kate.

Richard continued to stare. "Gabriel has been successful at everything he's ever touched. He's managed the family's finances successfully. I was given mine and it's already gone. He wanted to be an architect from the time he was three, and he is. One of the best. I still don't know what I want to be. He had a successful marriage—however short-lived it turned out to be. I have one-night stands. To tell you the truth, I think I'm jealous. But that only lasts for a few minutes, then I get over it." He looked at Kate. "Besides that, he's just no fun. I don't know what Carly sees in him."

"Speaking as a woman, I can tell you that he's very attractive."

"But hardly Carly's type."

"Maybe she's drawn to his maturity."

"Maybe."

Kate touched his arm. "Richard, are you in love with my sister?" she asked, a hint of sympathy in her voice.

Richard looked across the room at Carly. "I don't think so. I'm certainly attracted to her. Maybe it's love." He shrugged. "Who knows?"

"Have you told her?"

"Repeatedly." Then he corrected himself. "That I'm attracted, not that I'm in love."

"What did she say?"

"It's not what she said. It's her behavior. She likes having men fall all over her. She's used to it. So which guy does she choose to marry? The one who ignores her."

"In a weird way, that makes sense," said Kate.

"I know. But that doesn't make it any easier to take."

"So, you aren't sleeping with her?"

"Not since she got engaged to Gabriel."

Kate couldn't help the expression of distaste that crossed her expressive face.

Richard raised his hand. "I know, I know. I'm trying to be good now, though. It isn't easy."

Kate watched her sister as she animatedly chatted with a circle of men. She looked happy and Kate truly hoped she was.

She searched for Gabriel and found him talking to a man nearly as tall as he with dark hair in a businessman's cut, going gray at the sides. The man looked up and straight into her eyes. His expression was so odd... almost regretful.

"Who's that?" she asked Richard.

"Who's who?"

"The man speaking with your brother."

Richard turned in the direction Kate was looking. "That's his attorney, Harry Granville—and incidentally the host of the party."

Gabriel turned his head at that moment and looked at her.

Kate's heart caught.

Without taking his eyes from Kate's, he said something to the attorney, then began crossing the room toward her.

The nearer he drew, the harder her heart pounded.

A woman stepped in front of him and began talking. Gabriel reluctantly took his eyes from Kate, but she continued watching him. He was, without question, the most attractive man she'd ever met—not just because of his looks, but his seriousness. There was something about him that said this was a man whose love a woman could trust without question. Maybe she *was* just a little envious of Carly.

Carly walked up to Kate and stood beside her, her arm around her waist. "What are you thinking?"

"That you're a very lucky woman."

"Yes. He's not bad. Of course, he's not one to show his emotions. That's a little difficult for me to deal with, but I'll get used to it."

"As long as you know how he feels, it shouldn't matter if he shows it in public."

"I know."

"I imagine you're excited at the prospect of becoming a mother."

Carly glanced at Kate. "You met Willa?"

"Yes," said Kate with a smile. "She's a wonderful little girl. I met Mrs. Trent, too."

Carly let out a long breath.

"What's wrong?"

"The woman doesn't like me. She'd be the happiest person in the world if her grandson would call off this wedding."

"I didn't get that impression at all."

"Wait until you're around her a little more. That polite facade is bound to slip."

"If you feel this way now, how are you going to live under the same roof with her?"

"Once I'm in place as Gabriel's wife and Willa's stepmother, there won't be any need for Laurel Trent. She's served her purpose. She can go back to America."

"Does she know this?"

"I'll make it clear to her."

"What about Gabriel?"

"He'll go along with whatever I decide."

"I don't know, Carly. He doesn't strike me as being the kind of man who's going to send his grandmother away just because his wife tells him to."

Carly smiled. "You'll see."

Unnoticed by Kate, Richard had wandered off and now returned holding out a glass of soda. "Here you go, Kate. Another shot of caffeine."

She set her empty glass on a nearby table and gratefully took the new one. "Thank you."

"Did I miss anything?"

"Not much."

He looked at Carly as he sipped his drink. "Enjoying yourself?"

"Not particularly. I don't know very many people here."

"Better get used to it because this is going to be your life after you're married to my brother."

"On the contrary. Your brother's life will be in for some changes. I don't see us spending much time here. My work is mostly in London, Paris and New York. I'm sure he'll be traveling with me a great deal of the time."

"He has a career of his own," said Richard.

She just smiled. "You'll see."

Richard looked at her as though she'd lost her mind, but didn't say what he was thinking. Instead, he turned his attention to Kate. "Have you done any mingling?"

"Not yet."

"Want to?"

"Oh, I don't know. Socializing is a lot of work. I'm not sure I'm up to it this evening. I can barely string two sentences together."

"Take a big swig of your soda."

She did.

He took her free hand in his. "Now, come with me. I'll introduce you around."

Kate looked helplessly at Carly, but Carly's attention was already focused on someone else.

Kate allowed him to lead her to one group after another and she did the best she could to take part in the conversation. The people were, for the most part, very nice and clearly thought the world of Gabriel. Kate hoped that Carly would give them a chance in her new life as Mrs. Tent.

Gabriel's eyes followed Kate around the room. She was relaxed and confident and moved gracefully from group to group with Richard as her guide.

Kate could feel Gabriel's eyes on her and she found it disconcerting. Then she thought maybe it was her imagination working overtime, but as she was saying something to Richard, she looked over his shoulder, and there was Gabriel, twenty feet away, his shoulder leaning against a marble pillar, his arms crossed over his chest—his eyes on her.

Without realizing it, she'd stopped speaking in midsentence. Richard looked at her expectantly. "And?" he said.

She dragged her eyes from Gabriel and focused on Richard. "And what?"

"Finish what you were saying."

"I . . . I seem to have lost my train of thought."

"Brother, you really are fading fast. We should probably get you home."

"I'd appreciate that."

"Wait here. I'll talk to Gabriel."

Kate was determined not to look in Gabriel's direction. She looked everywhere but there. She spotted Carly standing in a quiet corner, deep in conversation with Harry Granville. She seemed angry. So did the attorney.

Her attention was distracted by a tall, thin woman in a stunning blue formfitting dress that shimmered in the light with every step she took. She walked straight to Kate and extended her hand. "You're Kate Fairfax. Richard told me to expect you. I'm Dee Granville."

Kate smiled at her and shook her hand. "Hello. Thank you so much for inviting me at the last minute."

"It was no problem, believe me. We always have room for one more at our parties. How are you enjoying your visit so far?"

"I've only been here since this afternoon, but I like it well enough."

"How long are you staying?"

"Until after the wedding. Then I have to get back to Chicago and my job."

"I think I recall Richard saying you work for a museum there."

"That's right."

"It must be fascinating."

Kate couldn't help smiling. "You're probably one of the few people who think that. And yes, I enjoy it very much." There were some people in the world you just automatically liked without knowing a thing about them. Dee was one of those people.

Dee was thinking the same thing about Kate and smiled at her. "I hope we get the chance to spend some time together before you leave."

"I'd like that." Kate was suddenly conscious of Gabriel standing behind her. Every nerve in her body went on alert.

"It's a good party, Dee." His voice was a smooth, deep rumble above Kate's ear.

Dee cocked an eyebrow. "Liar. You hate parties."

"I didn't say I liked it. I said it was a good one."

"So good that you're leaving, right?"

"Right."

"I don't think your bride-to-be is ready to go just yet."

Gabriel followed her gaze and saw Carly still huddled with Harry and still in a heated discussion. "Carly's a party animal. She'll be here until the wee hours. I, on the other hand, have things to do in the morning, and Kate here has already been up since yesterday."

"So you're just going to leave Carly here?"

"In Richard's capable hands. He doesn't mind, believe me."

"That's quite an attitude for a newly engaged man," said Dee.

"Carly's a big girl."

"Mm-hmm," said Dee skeptically.

Gabriel put his hand at Kate's waist. "You, on the other hand, are coming with me."

Her whole body tensed at his touch. "No," she said abruptly. "I'll stay here until Carly's ready to leave."

"You're tired. I can see it in your eyes."

"Well, yes, but—"

"So why would you want to stay?"

"I want to spend some time with my sister."

"Carly's ignored you all evening. That's not going to change."

"She's been preoccupied."

"If she wanted to be with you, she would have done it by now."

"I don't—"

"Come on," he said as he put gentle pressure on her waist and moved her toward the door. "You can talk to her tomorrow. Right now you look as though you're going to fall asleep standing up."

Kate gave in. She was too tired to argue. The short nap she'd taken in Willa's room had only made things worse. Besides, there was no reason to be afraid of Gabriel.

Of course, it wasn't Gabriel she was afraid of. It was her own reaction to him. But she was in control of that. She looked up at him with all of the confidence her tired psyche could muster. "You're right. Thank you. I'd really like to go home."

Chapter Five

As they stepped outside into the 1:00 a.m. darkness, Gabriel took off his tuxedo jacket and draped it around Kate's shoulders to ward off the early-morning chill. "Better?"

"Yes, thank you," said Kate as she pulled it more snugly around her and held it closed with her hands.

Gabriel placed his hand in the middle of her back as they walked. It was an innocent enough contact, but Kate was uncomfortably aware of his touch.

When they arrived at his car, Gabriel opened the unlocked passenger door for her.

Kate stood in front of him but made no move to get in. "I'm curious about something."

"What?"

"You're being nice enough to me now, but what was going on earlier? Why did you tell me I couldn't spend time with Willa?"

Gabriel hesitated before answering. "It's a long and complicated story."

"I have time."

"And it's none of your business."

"Ah," said Kate. "The party's over and it's back to square one for the two of us."

"No, not square one."

"So we're friends?"

"I don't think that describes us."

"What does?"

Gabriel looked at her for a long moment. "Tired. Get in the car, Kate."

"But—"

"Get in."

Kate dutifully climbed inside and he closed the door after her.

The ride home was silent, and that was all right with Kate. She sat quietly, her head against the back of her seat, eyes closed. The rich, low hum of the engine would have lulled her to sleep if they'd had farther to drive.

When the car stopped, Kate reluctantly opened her eyes and watched Gabriel walk around the front of the car. He opened her door and took her hand to help her out. As tired as she was, Kate still had to steel herself against the jolt his touch sent through her. She self-consciously let go of his hand as soon as she was on her feet, then looked at him to see if he'd felt the same thing.

Gabriel's expression was inscrutable.

"Thank you for taking me to the party and bringing me home. Quite honestly, I was glad to leave when we did. Good night."

She walked away, but Gabriel, after a momentary hesitation, called her name. "Kate?"

She reluctantly turned around.

"If you want to spend time with Willa while you're here, it's all right with me."

Her eyes reflected her surprise. Gabriel didn't seem to be the kind of man who changed his mind easily. "Thank you."

"I'd appreciate it, though, if you wouldn't allow her to become too attached. I don't want her to be hurt when you leave."

"I'll try to be careful of her feelings."

He gazed at her face feature by feature. She looked exactly like the woman he hated. But this was Kate, not Carly. And he knew in the same way his grandmother seemed to know that the two women were as different as different could be.

Kate smiled nervously and backed away from him toward the house. "I have to go. See you tomorrow."

"What's wrong?"

"Nothing," she said quickly. "Absolutely nothing. I'm just tired." She abruptly turned around and the jacket fell from her shoulders.

They both bent to pick it up at the same time and as they reached out, their hands touched. Kate pulled hers back as though she'd been burned.

Gabriel picked it up and straightened. "Are you always this jumpy when you're tired?"

"Always," she lied.

"Good, because I'd hate to think it was caused by something I'd done."

"Of course not," said Kate with a smile she knew perfectly well was tremulous but was helpless to do anything about. "Thanks for letting me use your jacket. Good night."

"Good night, Kate."

It was all she could do to walk, not run, into the house and across the foyer, unaware of Gabriel's eyes following her up the stairs.

When she got upstairs, Kate started to go to her room, but changed her mind and turned the other way to go to Willa's room. She pushed open the slightly ajar door on silent hinges. Crossing the room in the soft light of the dresser lamp, she saw that Willa had kicked off her covers. Kate pulled them up and tucked them more snugly around her. As she gazed at her, a wistful smile touching her lips, Kate's heart caught. She was such a beautiful little girl. She looked just the way Kate imagined her own daughter would have looked at this age.

She brushed Willa's hair away from her face with gentle fingers and let her hand rest for a moment on her forehead. "Sweet dreams," she whispered before quietly leaving.

In her own room, Kate undressed and pulled a nightgown out of her sister's shopping bag. It was floor-length white cotton with a ruffle around the hem and at the wrists. There was no shape to it, really. Yards of material floated around her. It wasn't Carly's kind of nightgown, but it suited Kate perfectly.

She picked up a brush and began her nightly ritual of pulling it through her hair, silently counting the strokes as she looked at herself in the mirror. The woman looking back seemed to belong to another era. Kate had felt that way so often, as though she belonged to another place, another time. That's what had drawn her to museums since childhood.

When she got to one hundred, she put the brush down, turned out the lights and tiredly sank onto the bed, pulling the covers up snugly around her.

Kate lay there, her eyes wide open, staring at the ceiling. She was exhausted, but her mind was racing.

She took a deep, relaxing breath and closed her eyes in a conscious effort to relax. Slowly she exhaled. Took another deep breath. Exhaled again.

It didn't work. Gabriel's face in all of its handsomely vivid detail kept appearing.

She turned onto her side and wrapped herself around a pillow, hugging it closely, and forced herself to think about other things. Her work. The book she was reading.

But Gabriel wouldn't be pushed aside. As soon as she stopped forcing her thoughts in different directions, his face came back. She could even hear his voice—deep and rich.

She punched the pillow into shape and flopped onto her stomach in frustration.

That didn't work.

She turned onto her back, awkwardly twisting the nightgown around her body.

She couldn't do this. She couldn't have feelings for this man. She wouldn't allow it.

"Ahhhhh!" she said aloud in frustration as she kicked off the blanket and sat straight up. There was nothing worse than trying to sleep when your mind wouldn't let you. The mind always won.

She could read, she thought.

Nah. Not in the mood.

She turned on the light next to the bed and sat there looking around. Then, with a sigh, she got up, walked to the window and held the drape back with her hand so she could look outside.

The moon shone on the sea, its lighted path rippling in the waves. That same light bathed the cliff and lawn. It was an eerie-looking combination of shadow and light that drew her to it.

Taking the blanket from the bed, Kate walked to her door and opened it a few inches so she could peer into the hallway. A light was on, but it was dim. No one was around.

On tiptoe, she quietly made her way down the long flight of stairs, opened the front door and stepped outside. It was a bit more brisk than it had been earlier. Walking around the house, her bare feet leaving prints on the damp grass, she went to the back and across the lawn to the spot she'd been looking at through her window.

As she stood there looking at the dark vastness of the water, Kate wrapped the blanket around her shoulders like a shawl to keep out the damp coolness of the night.

Raising her face to the sky, Kate let the salty wind sting her cheeks pink and whip her long hair around. She stood like a statue, her arms wrapped around herself, the bottom half of the nightgown billowing around her, its bright white visible in the moonlight against the backdrop of a velvety black sky.

Gabriel, as sleepless as Kate, stood in front of the French doors of his office looking outside. He didn't see Kate at first. She took form in his consciousness gradually in the moonlit shadows, a ghostly presence alone on the cliff.

She was so still.

He watched her for a long time and she never moved.

Gabriel opened the door and slowly crossed the lawn to Kate. He stood behind her.

Kate knew he was there, but this time she wasn't frightened. She turned her head, looked at him and smiled.

He didn't smile back. "What are you doing out here?"

"I couldn't sleep. What about you?"

"Same."

"It's so beautiful here."

Gabriel gazed out at the sea, black at this hour of the morning. "The view is the reason I bought the property."

She nodded. "I usually avoid anything to do with water, but I'm drawn to this."

"Why do you avoid it?"

"I'm afraid of it—probably because I can't swim. Either that or I can't swim because I'm afraid of the water."

"You should learn."

She nodded. "Gabriel?"

"Yes."

"Do you love my sister?" She turned her head to look at him. "I mean, do you really, deep down in your soul, can't live without her, love my sister?"

The muscle in his jaw tightened. "My feelings for your sister are personal."

"Of course. I'm sorry. I shouldn't pry. I just want to know in my heart that she's doing the right thing in marrying you. I want her to be happy."

"Are you afraid that she won't be with me?"

"I think so. She needs someone who loves her completely, holding nothing back. She needs to feel that love as though it's embedded in her very soul. I don't sense that from you when you're with her."

"I can't alter my behavior to ease your fears, Kate. I am the way I am." He turned her around to face him and pulled the blanket more snugly around her, holding it together with his hands as they rested between her breasts. "Or is your real concern that I'm not capable of the kind of love you've described?"

Her eyes looked into his. "I don't know why, but I think you are." She reached out from the blanket and raised her hand to his face, trailing the tip of her finger lightly over his scar. "How did you get this?"

Gabriel would normally have flinched from anyone touching him there, but not from Kate. "When I was young—twelve years old—the house we were living in caught fire. Everyone got out but my dog. I went back in after her through a broken window. The glass cut my face."

"Did you find her?"

He shook his head. "No."

"I'm sorry."

A corner of his mouth lifted. "It was a long time ago." His eyes moved over her face. "You should be in bed."

"I know. I couldn't sleep."

"Why?"

Kate lowered her eyes. "I was thinking too much."

"About?"

"Different things."

Gabriel reached out a gentle hand and cupped her cheek. He didn't even realize he was doing it until it was done.

Kate's heart flew straight into her throat.

"You're very different from your sister."

Kate nodded. "Carly has always been more outgoing and fun. That's her nature. I'm more inwardly focused and quiet. That's my nature. Kind of like you and your brother."

Gabriel trailed his thumb over her smooth, cold cheek, then let his hand fall to his side.

For Kate, the warmth of his touch lingered long after he took his hand away. As she stood there with him, her eyes moved slowly over his face. He took her breath away. Everything about him.

Gabriel watched her curiously. "You have a strange look on your face. What are you thinking?"

Kate looked away as she shifted the blanket. "Nothing important." Only that she was deeply attracted to the one man in the world she shouldn't be.

"Are you sure?"

Kate nodded. "You know, I think I'll go back to bed now. I'm suddenly feeling tired. Good night."

"Good night, Kate."

Gabriel watched her walk away until he couldn't see her any longer, then turned toward the sea, staring out but not really seeing it.

Kate went straight to her room and paced back and forth. This was terrible. How could she allow herself to be attracted to her sister's fiancé? It was completely unacceptable.

Still wrapped in the blanket, she lay down on the bed. She would get over it. She'd force herself to. No one need ever know. She would get through the next week and a half and leave for Chicago. It would all be over.

Kate closed her eyes tightly. Sleep. She needed sleep. That was probably where all of these unexpected feelings were coming from. Sleep deprivation.

This time it took only a few minutes for her to start drifting off. She was in that lovely in-between state, conscious and yet not conscious, dreaming but not dreaming.

She awakened abruptly to the sound of a loud crash. Sitting straight up, her heart hammering, her ears straining for any noise, Kate looked around her dark room and tried to orient herself.

She heard another noise—not a crash. More like a door closing somewhere down the hall.

Climbing out of bed, she tiptoed across her room and opened her door a crack. There was nothing in the dimly lit hallway.

Opening the door wider, she stepped out of her room and listened.

Nothing.

Walking to her sister's room, she opened the door and looked inside. Carly wasn't there, and her bed obviously hadn't been slept in, so it wasn't her.

Had she imagined the noise?

Back in the hall, she stood still and listened. There it was again, not as loud. She walked toward it, past her own room to a part of the house she hadn't been in before.

Again she heard the creaking noise of a door, then the click as it was quietly closed.

As she came to the corner, she moved closer to the wall and looked around the edge before venturing around herself. She was sure that was where the noise had come from.

There was only one door. Kate walked up to it, leaned her ear against it and softly knocked.

No one answered.

She knocked a little more firmly.

Still nothing.

Placing her fingers on the handle, she slowly pressed down until she could push the door open a crack. The room beyond was dark. "Hello," said Kate. "Is anyone in there?"

When there was no answer, she pushed it open farther so she could look inside. She was expecting a bedroom, but this clearly wasn't. And while it was dark, it wasn't pitch-black. She could make out that it was a small area, perhaps ten feet by ten. There was a spiral staircase in the center of it that rose three stories straight up to a skylight.

That explained why it wasn't completely dark, she thought. Moonlight.

With an outstretched hand, she searched the wall beside the door for a light switch, found one and flipped it. Nothing happened. She flipped it several more times, as though that would help. It didn't.

"Hello?" she called again as she moved toward the staircase. "Is anyone up there?"

Silence.

"Hello?" she called a little more loudly. "I know someone came in here. Please answer me."

Again, silence.

She stood there and waited, her senses alert.

Thump.

It was the tiniest of sounds, but Kate heard it. She moved to the staircase and put her hand on the railing. The sound had come from up there.

"Carly? Is that you?"

When they were children, Carly was constantly hiding in places and then jumping out at Kate to frighten her.

"Carly?" she said again. "Come on down. This isn't funny."

No one came.

Kate, lifting up the hem of her nightgown, began climbing up one step at a time. As she rounded the first curve, Kate saw the dull beam of what seemed to be a flashlight moving up even as she climbed.

Kate smiled. Now she knew it was Carly playing a trick.

"Come on, Carly. I'm on to you. Say something."

The light kept moving up and swinging back and forth as it went. Kate couldn't make anything else out.

Kate kept climbing, one hand holding up her nightgown, the other hand on the wooden railing.

She had rounded the second curve and was halfway up that when the light she'd been following went completely out. Kate couldn't see anything. She stopped climbing and stood absolutely still, her senses on alert.

This had definitely been a bad idea. If it was Carly playing a joke, it wasn't funny any longer.

As Kate turned to go back down the stairs, she heard a rustling sound that came closer and closer.

Something—or someone—brushed past her, shoving Kate hard into the railing. She screamed as she somersaulted over it, frantically reaching out to grasp something—anything. Her right hand wrapped around a vertical slat in the railing. She was dangling, but she still couldn't see anything.

The door she'd entered through opened and let in a sliver of light, then closed again and plunged the tower into darkness.

Kate was able to grasp a second vertical slat with her left hand and she struggled to pull herself up.

It was useless. She couldn't.

She was, she knew, nearly twenty feet up, and she was going to fall straight down.

Kate tried swinging her body so she could get her foot on one of the stairs. Back and forth.

She reached with her foot and missed completely. "Damn," she said under her breath.

Back and forth again.

This time she touched it with her toe. It gave her hope.

Her shoulders and arms were killing her. She was aware of every single muscle, straining and pulling.

Back and forth.

She almost had it when her right hand lost its grip completely and she was hanging on for dear life with only one hand clenched around the rounded slat.

Kate struggled to get a grip with her other hand, but the way the stairs were built, she couldn't reach anything without pulling up the weight of her body with that one hand, and her strength was rapidly draining from her arm.

Kate stopped moving. She could feel her grip slipping.

Chapter Six

The door below opened.

"Help me!" yelled Kate.

"I'm coming." It was Gabriel. He didn't ask any questions, but she could hear him taking the steps three at a time to get to her. He was there in the blink of an eye. With only the moonlight to help him see, Gabriel found her. First he grabbed her free hand and then wrapped his hand around the wrist of the hand she was hanging on with.

"Let go," he ordered.

Even before he said it, she lost her grip. If he hadn't been holding on to her, she would have fallen.

"I'm going to pull you up now," he said. "Don't struggle. Just keep your body limp."

She stopped moving and trusted him to pull her up.

He did. Quickly, although to Kate it seemed to take forever.

Gabriel pulled her onto the staircase and into his arms.

Kate, her whole body shaking, wrapped her arms around his neck and held on for dear life.

Gabriel held her close to his bare chest, his arms securely around her body. He buried his face in her hair. "Are you all right?"

She nodded.

He held her more tightly.

"I want to get out of here."

Without asking questions, Gabriel scooped Kate up in his arms and carried her down the stairs and out the door, all the way to her own room. He laid her down gently on her bed and sat beside her. Kate pulled herself into a sitting position and looked at her rescuer. "Thank you. I couldn't hold on any longer. How did you find me?"

"I heard you scream. What the hell happened?"

"I'm not sure."

"Start at the beginning."

She pushed her hair away from her face. "I was in bed, almost asleep, when I heard a noise. I went to see what it was or where it had come from and I heard it again. It led me to that place."

"The observatory."

"Is that what it is?"

"There's a big telescope at the top level."

"I didn't get that far. I opened the door thinking it was someone's room. Clearly it wasn't, but I was sure someone was in there. And they had a flashlight. I could see it moving as the person went up the steps. That's when it dawned on me that it was Carly playing a joke the way she had when we were children. So I went after her."

"Didn't you turn on the light so you could see who it was?"

"I tried to, but it didn't work. Anyway, I went up the stairs. I was about where you found me when I decided that maybe it wasn't Carly and this wasn't a joke, and had started back down when whoever it was rushed past me and knocked me over the railing."

"Deliberately?"

"I think so. It was too hard a shove to have been an accident or just someone trying to run away."

"And you don't have any idea who it was?"

"None. I couldn't see anything."

"And they ran out the door?"

"Yes."

"I was there within seconds of hearing you scream and I didn't see anyone coming out."

"Just because you didn't see anyone doesn't mean no one was there," she said defensively.

"True enough." His eyes moved over her face. "Are you all right, Kate?"

"Fine now, thanks to you."

"Okay. You stay here for a minute. I want to take a look at the observatory to see if I can find anything."

"Are you coming back?"

"In a few minutes."

Kate watched him walk away from her, his broad shoulders bare, wearing only drawstring pajama bottoms. Pulling her knees up under her chin and wrapping her arms around them, she waited, her eyes on the door he'd closed behind him.

Gabriel quickly covered the distance between Kate's room and the observatory. The door was open. He stepped inside and flicked the light switch.

Indirect but nonetheless bright light filled the area, and the lights built into each of the stairs glowed, as well.

As he moved toward the stairs, his eyes missed nothing, looking for anything that would indicate someone had been in there with Kate.

There was nothing.

He went up the stairs slowly, one at a time, all the way to the top. Nothing was disturbed. The telescope was in the same position he'd left it the day before.

Coming back down, he turned out the lights and closed the door behind him.

Kate was sitting in the same position when he returned to her, now wearing a T-shirt.

"Well?" she asked. "Did you find anything?"

He sat beside her again. "Only that the lights work."

"You're kidding."

"No. They all came on."

"That doesn't make sense. How could they be working now and not earlier?"

He tucked her hair behind her ear with a gentle hand. "Kate, are you sure there was someone else in there with you?"

Kate looked at him for a long moment, her distress obvious. "Don't you believe me?"

"I don't know. I think you're tired. Maybe your imagination is working overtime."

"I was there. I didn't dream that."

"True. But the lights work. And there's no one else there now, and no evidence there ever was."

"I know what happened," she said stubbornly.

"What's important is that you're all right now, however things happened. What you need to do now is sleep."

"I can't possibly."

A corner of his mouth lifted. "I'm a little wired myself. Come on downstairs with me and we'll have a drink. Maybe that'll relax us enough so we can sleep."

Kate put her hand in his and let him pull her from the bed. "That's a good idea."

Together they went downstairs. Gabriel took her to his office and while he went to the built-in bar, she walked around looking at things. There was a big desk with a computer at one end and a specially designed printer that could handle blueprint-sized paper.

She crossed the room to where a large tilted drawing board sat in front of some large windows, in a perfect position to catch natural light. There was an unfinished drawing of a multistoried office building along with the tools he'd been using to work on it.

"Where's this going to be?" she asked.

"Chicago."

Kate smiled. "Downtown?"

Gabriel brought her a small snifter of brandy and stood beside her as she looked at his drawing. "Yes. It's going to replace a hotel that was torn down about a year ago."

"So this is a hotel, too?"

"Yes."

"It's going to be beautiful."

"And functional. These days people can't really afford one without the other."

"Does that make it more difficult to design?"

"It's more of a challenge," he agreed, "but I enjoy it."

"It'll be fun having one of your buildings where I live. I can tell people that I know the architect."

Gabriel smiled. "Do you mind if I work while we try to make ourselves tired?"

"Of course not. I'll just enjoy what's left of the fire." Kate moved around the drawing board to the middle of the spacious room where there was a large, comfortable-looking leather couch and chairs on an Oriental rug. A fire burned low in the fireplace, giving off a little warmth and a cozy glow. Kate sank onto the couch with a sigh and took a sip of the brandy. The first sip burned on the way down, but it felt good. She took another sip and then placed the snifter on the large, round coffee table and stretched out on the couch, one arm behind her head, as she looked at the fire.

Gabriel sat on the stool in front of his drawing board and clicked on the attached lamp, bending it to focus its beam on his work.

"I used to sleepwalk," said Kate.

Gabriel looked up. "What?"

She turned her head so she could see him. "When I was a child, I used to sleepwalk. I'd wake up in some of the strangest places. Sometimes I'd have cuts and bruises and have no idea how I'd gotten them. I outgrew it when I was a teenager. But maybe not altogether. That could be what happened tonight."

"Do you think it is?"

"I don't know. Could I have dreamed the noise and the push?"

"Did it seem like a dream at the time?"

"No. It was very real."

"I'll take another look tomorrow. Maybe I missed something."

A smile curved her mouth. "Thanks."

Gabriel went back to his drawing and Kate went back to looking at the dying fire.

He looked at her a couple of minutes later and she was sound asleep. With a smile, he went to the chair next to her, took the folded blanket from the armrest and spread it over her.

As he was leaning over her to pull up the blanket, Kate opened her eyes and smiled. "Thank you."

"You're welcome," he said softly. "Go back to sleep."

She already had.

Gabriel went back to his board, but he spent more time looking at Kate than he did working.

Putting down his pencil, he picked up his brandy and walked to the couch. Sliding her snifter to one side, he sat on the coffee table and leaned forward, his elbows on his knees, holding his brandy between his two cupped hands. Kate's face was turned toward him.

Gabriel intensely examined her every feature in minute detail. She had the kind of face no one would describe as cute, but everyone would see as beautiful. Her forehead was smooth, her eyebrows the same auburn as her lush hair curved over softly beautiful, thickly lashed eyes. Her cheekbones were defined, her nose straight. Her lips were full, but not artificially so. And there was a hint of a dimple even in her sleep at the right corner of her mouth. Her skin was pale and smooth.

He reached out a gentle finger and drew it down her cheek. It felt as soft as it looked.

With a shake of his head, Gabriel tossed back the rest of his brandy in one shot, then leaned over the couch to pick up Kate.

She stirred and opened her eyes. "What's going on?"

"Go back to sleep. I'm carrying you to bed."

"I can walk," she said groggily, even as she closed her eyes and went back to sleep.

With a smile, Gabriel lifted her in his arms and held her high against his heart. She moved slightly and brought her right hand to rest lightly on his chest.

He carried her out of his office and up the stairs to her room, laying her on the bed and pulling the covers up over her.

"Good night," she mumbled without opening her eyes.

"Good night, Kate," he said softly.

Carly had come up the stairs behind Gabriel and Kate and now stood in the doorway of the bedroom, her arms crossed over her breasts, her expression angry. "What are you doing here?" she asked loudly.

"Lower your voice. Kate's sleeping."

"Which doesn't answer my question. What are you doing here?"

"Your sister had a scare earlier. She's all right now, though."

"What kind of scare?"

Gabriel straightened away from Kate and turned to face Carly. "She thinks someone tried to push her over the railing in the observatory."

A grin split Carly's face. "You're kidding."

"No."

"Leave it to Kate to come up with something like that."

"She nearly fell, Carly."

Carly shrugged.

"I see you're as loving toward your sister as you are toward everyone else."

"Kate can take care of herself."

"She thinks she might have been sleepwalking."

"She probably was. She did it all of the time when we were kids. As soon as she got upset about something, you could count on Kate taking a midnight stroll.''

Gabriel looked back at the bed.

Carly moved farther into the room. "You seem awfully concerned about her, considering she's my sister."

He didn't say anything.

"If you think you can get to me through Kate," she said in a hushed voice meant for his ears only, "you're mistaken. Don't even try it."

"Not everyone uses people the way you do, Carly."

"Sure, they do. I'm just honest about it."

"Go to bed, Carly."

She turned to leave the room, but paused in the doorway. "You might as well get used to the idea of marriage to me because there's no way you're going to get out of it."

"We'll see."

Carly smiled and went to her room.

Chapter Seven

Kate awoke to the feeling she was being stared at. When she opened her eyes, she found Willa standing next to her bed.

"Good morning," said Kate in surprise.

"Good afternoon," said Willa with a smile. "I've been waiting for you to wake up for hours."

Kate raised up on her elbows. "Why? What's going on?"

"Dad and I are going to a carnival today and we want you to come with us."

"Oh, Willa, I'm sorry, but I think I should stay here with my sister to help her with wedding preparations."

"She's not here."

"Do you know where she went?"

Willa shrugged. "She left a little while ago with Uncle Richard. My dad might know if you want to ask him."

"It's not important."

"So you'll go with us?"

Kate couldn't help smiling. She really didn't think she should be spending the day with Gabriel and Willa—particularly Gabriel—but she didn't know how to gracefully get out of it. "Can you wait long enough for me to take a shower and get dressed?"

"Sure, but hurry."

"I will."

Willa skipped out the door. Kate quickly rose, showered and dressed in a pair of Carly's jeans, which were too tight for comfort, and a T-shirt that fit like a glove and left her midriff bare. Kate looked in the mirror and clicked her tongue. This wouldn't do at all.

Bending over, she went through the shopping bags looking for something more conservative to wear but, if anything, the clothes were more revealing. She was stuck with what she was wearing.

Hurrying to Carly's room, she looked through her closet for a blouse or sweater. Nothing. Clearly Carly had moved only a few suitcases of her clothes here, and most of those were dresses along the line of what she'd worn the night before and some T-shirts that were smaller than the one she had on.

Kate looked at herself in the mirror again and sighed. The outfit just wasn't her. But it was all she had.

Feeling self-conscious about her exposed midriff, she went downstairs and found Gabriel and Willa waiting for her in the foyer.

Gabriel, who had been smiling at something Willa said, looked up when Kate appeared. His smile faded as he watched her walk down the stairs. "Sorry I took so long," she apologized. "Would there be a jacket around that I could borrow?"

Gabriel walked to a coat closet just off the foyer. Kate could hear the hangers as he moved them on the rack. A moment later he emerged with a bright red nylon windbreaker. "Will this do?"

"That's perfect, thank you." She gratefully took it from his outstretched hand, slipped her arms into the sleeves and zipped it up so that her midriff was covered.

Willa put her hand in Kate's. "You're going to like the carnival," she said as they walked outside into the sunny afternoon. "It's run by Gypsies. They come every year."

"And do you go with your dad every year?"

"Yes. I like the rides."

"What's your favorite one?"

She thought for a moment. "The Ferris wheel. Have you ever been on one?"

"Not since I was about your age."

"Will you go with me?"

"Of course. I'd love to."

Gabriel walked to the black four-wheel-drive vehicle and opened the rear and passenger doors. "Come on, girls. Let's go."

Willa jumped into the back and immediately strapped herself in. Kate was a little slower, but this time grabbed her seat belt before Gabriel could lean in to help her. He closed both doors, walked around to the driver's side and, once he'd gotten the car started, backed out.

Kate relaxed in her seat and watched the scenery go by as they made their way down the winding road. She could get used to rural England. It was beautiful and restful. No wonder Gabriel lived here.

Gabriel.

Kate glanced at his dark profile, then looked away. She'd learned as a child to push her feelings aside and carry on with what had to be done. This was no different.

They drove past a gently rolling farm where cows grazed beneath the watchful eye of an old stone house. Not far from there, they crossed over a freshly painted wood bridge that spanned a small stream. A fisherman in hip boots stood in the middle, fishing pole in hand.

"I can see why you like living here," said Kate. "I imagine it's going to be difficult after your marriage to change from this to living most of the year in larger cities."

"What are you talking about?"

"So you can be with Carly when she's working."

"I don't think so."

Kate turned her head. "How are you going to spend time together if you don't?"

"Look, Kate, I don't know what your sister told you, but I have no intention of changing my life because of her work. This is my home. This is where I intend to raise my daughter."

"I'm sorry," said a chastened Kate. "I must have misunderstood what Carly said."

Gabriel took a deep breath as he took his eyes off the road to look at her. "I didn't mean to snap at you."

"That's all right."

"No, it isn't. I've been losing my temper a lot lately with people who deserve better than that from me."

"It's probably nerves. Marriage is a little frightening."

He smiled, but there was no amusement in it. "Have you ever been married?"

"No. I don't think I ever will."

Gabriel glanced at her. "Why not?"

"I haven't found anyone who comes close to being the kind of man I want to spend the rest of my life with."

"Perhaps your standards are too high."

"Maybe. But I'm certainly not going to lower them."

"You'd rather be alone?"

"There's nothing wrong with being alone. I have my work and my friends and, as shocking as some might find it, I actually enjoy my own company."

"Interesting."

"What is?"

"That our outlooks are so similar."

"With a difference. You've found someone to spend your life with."

Kate was watching his profile. She saw his jaw clench and unclench. "Did I say something wrong?"

"Look, you can see the Ferris wheel from here," he said, changing the subject.

Willa leaned forward as much as her seat belt would allow. "Dad, may I have some cotton candy when we get there?"

"Of course. What's a carnival without cotton candy?"

As they got closer, Kate could see that the carnival had been set up on a stretch of open, grassy land. Cars were parked haphazardly on the grass. There were colorful mobile homes lined up hood to bumper near the game booths.

Gabriel found a parking place about a hundred feet from the entrance. Willa was out of the car and running toward the carnival before Kate had even undone her seat belt. Gabriel opened his door and called to her. "Willa, wait for us."

So Willa stopped, doing everything but hopping in place to let them know how impatient she was.

Gabriel and Kate walked quickly to catch up with her. She skipped between the two of them, holding their hands. To anyone watching, they were the perfect family.

Tinkling music filled the air, one song fading into another as they walked past some of the rides. A man on stilts wearing yellow patchwork trousers held up by bright red suspenders politely doffed his hat as he walked past them.

A woman in a bright bandanna approached them with a camera. "Would you like to have your picture taken?"

"Yes!" said Willa.

Gabriel lifted Willa in his arms while Kate moved toward the photographer so she could watch.

"What are you doing?" asked Gabriel.

"Getting out of the way."

"Get back here. The three of us are here, so the picture should reflect that."

"Really, I . . ."

Still carrying Willa, Gabriel stepped forward to grasp Kate's hand and pull her to his side.

"I want to be in the middle," said Willa.

Gabriel shifted her to his other side. Willa put a slight arm around his neck and her other arm around Kate's. "Ready?" he asked her.

"Yes." Willa looked straight into the camera and smiled while both Kate and Gabriel were looking at Willa and smiling. The camera flashed. The woman handed Gabriel a card with a number on it. "If you come to the tent by the exit in about an hour, the picture will be ready for you to buy."

Gabriel set Willa on her feet as he pocketed the card. "Where to now?"

"The Ferris wheel," said Willa, grabbing her father's hand and dragging him behind her.

"Come on," he called to Kate, holding out his hand.

She ran to catch up and slipped her hand into his. When they got there, they stood in line with a dozen other people. Gabriel bought the tickets and immediately handed them to the man watching the wheel. All three of them fit in one of the swinging seats with Willa in the middle. Gabriel pulled down the safety bar, then rested his arm along the back of the seat. Kate felt his fingertips brush against her shoulder.

The Ferris wheel jerked, and they went halfway up when it stopped again to let on more passengers. It did this a few more times, leaving them swinging in the air, their legs dangling, with a wonderful view of the rest of the carnival and the surrounding countryside.

Willa's pretty face was lit with excitement as the great wheel began to go around and around. And Kate, watching her, couldn't remember ever being quite so happy. Smiling, she looked up and straight into Gabriel's eyes. Her heart slammed against her ribs.

Gabriel, watching Kate even as she watched his daughter, wondered what it was he was feeling for this woman he'd met just the day before. Her resemblance to Carly was still startling. But the more time he spent with her, the less the resemblance mattered. He was attracted to Kate, yet he'd never been attracted to Carly.

As Kate looked into his eyes, her smile slowly faded. They sat there, gazes locked, oblivious to everything around them.

As the giant wheel slowed to a crawl and then stopped, Kate and Gabriel self-consciously looked away from each other. They were the first to get off the ride. Again, Willa was in the middle, holding each of their hands, swinging them back and forth as they strolled along the midway. They stopped to buy popcorn for Gabriel and cotton candy for Willa and Kate.

When they got to the merry-go-round, Gabriel bought a ticket for Willa, went through the line with her and helped her onto a unicorn. She handed him her cotton candy. "Promise you won't eat it?"

"You have my word as a gentleman."

Willa grinned at him, then waved at Kate as Gabriel left the carousel and came to stand next to her.

Kate pinched off a bite of her own cotton candy and put it in her mouth, letting it melt on her tongue. "This is *sooo* bad for me," she said with relish.

Gabriel looked at her and smiled. "You sound as though you're enjoying it."

"Completely. At this rate, though, I'll never be able to fit into Carly's jeans."

"You don't need to."

As the carousel came full circle, Willa waved until she disappeared, only to start waving again as soon as she came into view. Gabriel and Kate waved back.

"She's a happy child," said Kate.

"I think she was born happy," said Gabriel. "From the first moment she came to us she's been a smiler." He looked down at Kate. "I'm glad to see you're all right after last night."

"I'm fine. Just a little tired. I had a hard time getting to sleep after that."

"Any more thoughts on what might have happened?"

She shook her head.

"I spoke with Carly last night. She confirmed what you said about sleepwalking."

"As far as I know, I haven't done that since I was ten."

"Maybe the jet lag caused you to do it again."

"Meaning that no one was there at all?"

"That's right. It could be that you simply awoke suddenly on the staircase and lost your balance."

"I don't know. It still bothers me that I remember hearing the noise and climbing the stairs in the first place. Before, when I was sleepwalking, I never remembered anything."

"Maybe it's different when you're an adult."

"Maybe." Kate was silent for a moment. "I don't know. In the harsh light of day, whatever reality I thought was there last night seems to have faded into obscurity."

"If it's any consolation, I checked the tower again this morning. There was no sign that anyone else had been there—although I don't know what 'signs' would have been left behind. Of course, if rumor is to be believed, the house is haunted. Maybe a ghost got you."

Kate smiled at his ridiculous suggestion. "I think I prefer the sleepwalking explanation."

"I thought you might. Give me a bite."

"What?"

"Of your cotton candy. I promised Willa I wouldn't eat hers."

Kate pinched some off between her thumb and forefinger and held it to his lips.

Gabriel caught her wrist in his hand. As he took the cotton candy between his strong white teeth, his lips brushed her fingertips.

Kate felt the reaction all the way to her toes. She quickly pulled her wrist away and lowered her eyes so he wouldn't see, but it was too little too late. Gabriel had seen all too clearly what she would have hidden.

The carousel coming to a stop saved the day. Willa jumped off her unicorn and ran to them. "What now?" she asked.

"Whatever you want, sweetheart," said Gabriel, a warm smile lighting his eyes.

She took her cotton candy from his hand.

There was a colorful tent, its flaps open just enough to see inside. A woman dressed in full Gypsy costume sat at a small table covered by an elaborately fringed cloth with a crystal ball in front of her.

Gabriel inclined his head toward the tent. "Want to have your fortune told?"

"I don't think so," said Kate with a smile.

"I do! I do!" cried Willa. "Please? You too, Kate."

Gabriel bought tickets and all three of them went inside. Willa sat down first in a folding chair across from the woman. The woman looked at them all with a friendly smile. "So," she said as she covered the crystal ball with a deep red napkin-sized square of cloth, "you want to look into your future, little one?"

"Yes, please."

"Let's see what we find." She uncovered the ball, which was now lit from within. "Mmm," she said, nodding.

"What?" asked Willa as she scooted to the edge of her seat.

"I see great happiness for you. A good friend who moved away will be returning."

Willa turned to her father with happy eyes. "Cristina! Our teacher said she was coming back."

"I also see a change occurring in your family."

"My dad's getting married."

The woman nodded and continued to gaze into the crystal ball. A frown creased her forehead and grew deeper. "But not to the woman he thinks he's marrying." She seemed genuinely confused as she looked first at Gabriel and then at Kate. "Things are not as they seem—to anyone involved."

But Willa wasn't interested in that. "Can you tell if I'm going to get a pony?"

Again she gazed into her ball. "I don't see a pony, but I do see a dog. Small at first and then very large."

"I *love* dogs!" squealed Willa.

"And I see that someone you thought was lost to you forever will be back in your life."

"Who?"

"Someone close to you." She leaned back in her chair. "More than that, I can't see."

Willa got up, her eyes sparkling with excitement. "Christina's coming back and I'm getting a dog!"

Gabriel rested his hand on her shoulder. "Don't get your hopes up, Willa. Crystal balls have been known to make mistakes."

The woman looked at him with a raised dark brow. "Not mine." She waved Kate into the chair. "Now for you."

Kate reluctantly sat down while Willa and Gabriel stood behind her and watched.

"I see two of you," said the woman. "You are a twin?"

Kate couldn't have been more surprised. "Yes."

She nodded. "There is bad blood between the two of you."

"No," said Kate in surprise. "Not at all."

The woman looked up and into Kate's eyes. "Perhaps you are not aware of it, but trust me when I tell you that there is." She turned her attention back to the crystal ball and didn't say anything for several seconds. When she at last looked at Kate again, there was genuine concern in her eyes. "You must be very careful over the next few days."

Kate blinked in surprise. She'd been expecting her to say something she could say to everyone, like maybe she was the one who was going to get the pony, or find true love or some other such nonsense. This was spooky. "Careful of what?"

The woman glanced at Gabriel then quickly covered up her crystal ball with the cloth. "I'm sorry. I don't see anything else."

"Nothing?" asked Kate. "That's it?"

"It's finished."

"But..."

"You must leave now!" She rose so abruptly that she nearly knocked over her chair.

Until that moment, if you'd asked her, Kate would have said she didn't believe in crystal balls. But there was something in the way the woman was behaving that frightened her. It was as though she'd seen some terrible truth; a truth too horrible to say aloud.

And it was Kate's truth.

COMING NEXT MONTH

Chapter Eight

The woman was firm. "If you're not satisfied with my work, the man standing outside the tent will refund your money."

Clearly they were being dismissed.

Kate and Gabriel shared a look and a shrug as they walked outside. Gabriel didn't bother asking for his money back. "That was different," he said as they once again wandered down the midway.

"Eerie."

"What was that business about your having to be careful over the next few days?"

"Maybe I'm going to go flying over another banister."

Kate's tone was light, but that didn't alter the fact that the Gypsy's fright had communicated itself very clearly to her and left her feeling nervous.

"Let's hope not," said Gabriel. "Still, that's odd. I wonder what she meant."

"You know as much as I do. You know what's really strange, though? How did she know I had a twin?"

"Lucky guess?"

"The chances of that are fairly slim, but it's the only answer I can think of at the moment."

"Come on," said Willa impatiently as she tugged on their hands. "Walk faster."

The three of them spent the next two hours wandering the midway, going on rides, playing the carnival games. Gabriel won a big panda bear for Willa and a baby tiger for Kate.

Kate, except for the weird incident with the Gypsy, was having a wonderful time.

The last ride Willa wanted to go on was called The Rocket. In fact, nothing there looked like a rocket. It was a child's ride, with two-seater, bodylike jet capsules attached to spokes that turned in circles and went up and down.

"You two go ahead," said Kate.

"You can ride in the one behind us," said Willa.

Kate leaned over and kissed the top of her head. "Thank you, sweetheart, but I'm a little thirsty. While you and your dad are on the ride, I think I'll get myself a soda."

"Okay." She slipped her tiny hand into her father's large one, and off they went.

Kate watched from behind the fence as Gabriel lifted Willa into her seat and then climbed in behind her. She loved watching him with his daughter. All of his reserve fell away and left only tenderness. How lucky for Willa that this was the man who had chosen her for his daughter.

"Miss," hissed a voice from somewhere behind her.

Kate turned around in surprise.

"Over here."

It was the fortune-teller, standing behind the small ticket booth. Kate walked toward her. "What is it?"

"I couldn't tell you all that I saw in front of the others. You must be very, very careful."

"You said that before. Careful of what?"

"Someone close to you means you harm."

"Don't be ridiculous." Kate would have turned away, but the woman reached out and caught her arm.

"Please listen to me. You and your child are in grave danger. You now, and your child when you are no longer there to protect her."

Kate felt as though she'd taken a knife in her heart. "My child is dead."

"You're wrong. She's very much alive."

Kate removed the woman's hand from her arm. "You're a sick woman. Go away."

But the woman persisted. "Everything is not as it seems. That which you thought was true is not. You must trust no one but yourself." She looked over Kate's shoulder. "God be with you," she said quickly, then turned and ran.

Gabriel came up behind Kate and put his hand on her shoulder. "What was that all about?"

Kate shook her head, beyond words.

He turned Kate to face him. "You're trembling. What did she say to upset you like this?"

"Nothing. I don't want to talk about it."

Without thinking about what he was doing, Gabriel pulled Kate to him and held her in the safe circle of his arms. "We'll leave now. She won't bother you any more."

Kate pressed her hands against his chest. "I'm all right. She's just a silly woman with nothing better to do than harass people." Kate looked up at him and managed a hint of a smile. "What now?"

"You're sure you're all right?"

Kate nodded as she moved farther away from him. Farther away from his protective arms. "I overreacted. Something I seem to be doing a lot of lately."

Gabriel didn't look at all convinced. "Let's call it a day and get out of here."

Willa came up beside Kate and took her hand. "Where's your soda?" she asked.

"I didn't get one after all," she said with a smile, doing her best to push the fortune-teller's frightening words from her mind. "I wasn't as thirsty as I thought."

Gabriel took her other hand as they walked. By the time they got back to the car, it was a little after four. Gabriel settled Willa into the back, securely strapping her in, then opened the door for Kate.

"Thank you."

Gabriel opened the driver's door and paused. "I'll be right back," he said suddenly. "I forgot something."

Kate turned in her seat and looked back at Willa while they waited. Her cheeks were rosy, her beautiful hair windblown. To Kate's surprise, Willa took off her seat belt, reached out and wrapped her arms around Kate's neck. "I wish you were going to marry my dad."

"Thank you, sweetheart." Kate was truly touched and hugged her back. "But when you get to know Carly better, you'll be happy to have her as your new mom."

"Are you going to stay here after they're married?" she asked hopefully.

"I'm afraid not. I have to go back to my own home where my work is and my friends live."

"You could get a job here and make new friends."

Kate tweaked her nose. "Nice try."

Willa sat back in her seat with a look on her face only a child could achieve. "Will you visit sometimes?"

"If you'd like me to. And maybe you can come to Chicago to visit me."

"Really?"

"Absolutely."

The driver's door opened and Gabriel climbed into the car. "I'm back," he said as he started the engine. "Willa, put your seat belt on."

She hugged her dad, then did what he said.

Kate settled into her seat.

"Are you guys hungry?" he asked as he put the car into gear and headed for the road.

"Starving," said Kate.

"Good. Mrs. Meredith packed us a lunch so we could have a little picnic." He turned his head and looked at Kate. "I know Willa likes picnics. How about you?"

"It sounds wonderful."

Gabriel smiled at her and Kate melted.

While he focused on his driving, Kate watched his hands on the steering wheel. They were definitely a man's hands—long fingered and strong looking.

She had no idea how long she'd been staring at them when Gabriel pulled the car off to the side of the road and put it in Park. "This is the spot," he said.

They all climbed out of the car. Gabriel went around to the back, lifted the rear gate and took out a picnic hamper.

The three of them walked across a grassy meadow to a spot under a tree where they could look at the sea. Kate helped him spread a blue-and-white-checked cloth on the ground, then knelt in front of the hamper and began taking things out. There was freshly baked bread, sausage, cheese, apples, wine and juice.

They each prepared their own plate. Gabriel poured Kate and himself a glass of wine, and juice for Willa.

The little girl sat cross-legged with her plate on her lap and ate hungrily. Kate was hungry, too, and the bread was delicious.

Gabriel stretched out on his side, leaning on one elbow, and looked at the sea as he bit into an apple.

It was a beautiful afternoon, just warm enough to be comfortable. Willa finished eating and wanted to go exploring, so Kate cleared away her plate and looked at Gabriel. "Do you want to go?"

"No," he said, rolling onto his back and looking up at Kate. "I think I'll just lie here and enjoy the quiet."

Willa tugged on Kate's hand. "Come on."

And so, with some reluctance that she knew she shouldn't be feeling, Kate got to her feet and wandered off with Willa, looking at flowers and butterflies; listening to birds and waves; picking up pretty, smooth rocks and putting them in their pockets. They were gone for more than an hour. When they got back to Gabriel, he was sound asleep.

Willa leaned against Kate.

"Don't tell me you're sleepy, too," whispered Kate.

Willa nodded.

"All right. Let me clear a place for you."

She moved the basket to the side. Willa lay down with her panda bear and curled onto her side. With a smile, Kate took off her jacket and draped it over the child, then lay on her stomach between the two of them, her chin on her hands, and watched them sleep.

Willa was turned away from her, but Gabriel's head was turned toward her. Kate rested her cheek on the backs of her hands and just looked at him, her eyes slowly moving over the architecture of his face feature by feature. He wasn't what she would have called handsome in a classical sense, and yet he was one of the handsomest men she'd ever seen, scar or no scar.

Her eyes continued their trip over his strong neck and shoulders. He was a powerful man, tall and strong. She now knew from experience that having his arms around her made her feel safer than she'd ever felt in her life.

As her eyes journeyed on, over his flat stomach and strong thighs; she was unaware that Gabriel had opened his eyes and was watching her scrutiny with a serious tawny gaze.

Kate's eyes retraced their path over his body, coming to rest briefly on his mouth and then his eyes.

Eyes that were looking back at her.

Kate's cheeks flushed ever so slightly with embarrassment. "How long have you been watching me?"

"I'd have to say not nearly as long as you've been watching me," said Gabriel.

"Sorry."

Their faces were only a foot apart. Gabriel reached out with a gentle hand and touched her cheek.

Kate put her hand over his. "Don't," she said softly.

A corner of his mouth lifted, creasing a cheek already showing signs of late-afternoon shadow. He took his hand away. "Tell me something about yourself."

"Such as?"

"Why do you work in a museum rather than as a model?"

"I love beautiful things—old things. I did a little modeling when I was younger, but it didn't fulfil me and I'm afraid I wasn't very good at it. I prefer my work now."

"Have you ever been in love?"

"Once, I think."

"Don't you know?"

"I was very young. I'm not sure what I was feeling."

"I think if it was love you would have known it then and you'd know it now."

"Perhaps."

"So why aren't you in love now, Kate?"

"That's an odd question."

"Can you answer it?"

"There is no answer. One is either in love or one isn't. There's no particular reason for either state."

"Do you want to be?"

"I don't think so," she said thoughtfully. "It takes more energy than I have at the moment."

The two of them continued to look at each other, their faces close. "You have beautiful eyes," said Gabriel. "Very expressive."

"Too expressive," said Kate wryly. "People can always tell exactly what I'm thinking."

"What are you thinking at this moment?"

"That I like lying here like this talking to you, but shouldn't be doing it."

"Why not?"

"It's a little too intimate."

"Are you afraid I'll do something?"

"No. You aren't that kind of man."

"How do you know?"

"I can tell. You would never do anything to betray the woman you love, whatever the circumstances."

"So you're good at reading people?"

"Some. Not all." She raised her hand to his cheek. "You need to shave."

"I always do at this time of day." He felt her fingers brush the scar. "You asked me about my scar last night. Does it bother you?"

"No. It makes your face less perfect and more interesting." She took her hand away.

Gabriel's gaze came to rest on Kate's lips.

Her heart started beating a rapid tattoo beneath her breast. She quickly pushed herself into a sitting position. "We should probably be leaving."

Gabriel reluctantly sat up and watched as Kate went into her efficient mode. "We need to clean all of this up."

As she leaned over to pick up the basket, Gabriel covered her hand with his. "We didn't do anything wrong, Kate."

She didn't look at him. "I know."

"Thinking about wanting to do something and doing it are two very different things."

"I don't know what you're talking about," she said as she pulled her hand away and continued packing.

"Are you saying you didn't want me to kiss you just now?"

"You're my sister's fiancé."

"I'm only too well aware of my current position in Carly's life. That's not the issue."

Kate sat cross-legged across from him, her blue eyes full of distress. "That's exactly the issue, Gabriel. Thoughts can be as big a betrayal as actions."

"In other words," he said, "your eyes didn't lie. You did want me to kiss you."

"It doesn't matter because it isn't going to happen."

"I know."

"I don't want to talk about this anymore."

"There's something going on between us, Kate, and not talking about it isn't going to make it go away."

She shook her head as she moved away from him. "Carly and Richard are probably back by now. You carry Willa to the car while I fold the tablecloth and get the basket."

Gabriel sat up. "Kate..."

"Please, Gabriel. Don't."

Doing as she asked, he got up, then leaned over and lifted his daughter in his arms. "Come on, Willa," he said softly.

Kate methodically folded the tablecloth edge over edge. Maybe, she thought as she packed it into the basket, this was what had happened between Carly and Jeff. She had never understood it until this moment. The difference was that they had gotten to a point where they couldn't turn back.

But Kate wasn't Carly, and Gabriel wasn't Jeff.

From now on, her contact with Gabriel would be formal and infrequent. Nothing like what happened today would ever happen again.

Not ever.

Chapter Nine

So this was a family dinner at the Trent home, thought Kate.

She sat in the salon and people-watched. Laurel was sitting in her favorite chair working on her needlepoint. Gabriel was standing at the far end of the room, a half-empty glass in his hand, staring outside. Carly and Richard were seated on a couch, talking softly and laughing.

And Willa, all scrubbed after her day at the fair, was dressed up for dinner and sitting on the floor at a low, square table with a coloring book and crayons.

Kate's eyes came to rest on Gabriel's back. The more she watched him, the more curious she grew. He didn't act like a man who was in love and about to marry the

woman he wanted to spend the rest of his life with. He barely looked at Carly. In fact, he seemed to go out of his way to avoid looking at her.

And Carly. She couldn't begin to figure out her behavior. It seemed designed to antagonize Gabriel. Or perhaps make him jealous. That made a little sense. It didn't, however, appear to be working.

Laurel Trent looked over her half glasses at Kate. She saw very clearly in Kate's eyes what Kate probably wasn't even aware of herself.

And Gabriel.

Sighing to herself, she went back to her stitching. She was getting too old for this.

Carly, still talking to Richard, looked at her sister from the corner of her eye. It was clear where her sister's attention lay. Patting Richard on the leg, she rose and crossed the room to Gabriel, leaning against him, her arm around his waist, her cheek on his shoulder.

Gabriel's back went rigid.

Kate watched in surprise. Unless she was very wrong about what she was seeing, he didn't want Carly touching him.

But Carly moved even closer. "Did you enjoy your outing with my sister?" she asked in a low voice that only Gabriel could hear.

"Go away, Carly," said Gabriel. "I don't want to deal with you right now."

"You don't have a choice."

He took a long drink.

"What exactly did you and my sister do today?"

"What are you talking about?"

"I haven't seen her looking this love-struck since she was a teenager. Maybe not even then."

"What your sister feels and for whom she feels it is none of my business."

"I'd say it's very much your business."

"Is there a point to this conversation?"

"There's a point to all of my conversations with you."

"Then get to it."

"Keep your hands off my sister. As far as she's concerned, you belong to me. You and Willa both."

Gabriel was silent.

"After years of looking at her life and wishing it were mine, it's her turn to look at my life and wish it were hers."

"That gives you pleasure?"

Her mouth curved into a bitter smile. "You have no idea how much."

Gabriel gave Carly his full attention. "Are you doing all of this to get back at your sister for something?"

"Don't be ridiculous. I've already told you that I want to be married so that Willa can have both her biological mother in her life and keep you as her father."

But Gabriel hadn't bought that explanation before and he certainly wasn't buying it now.

Fully aware of her audience, Carly made a show of rubbing her cheek against his shoulder. "You might not know it yet—and you might not even believe that

it's possible, but you're eventually going to fall in love with me. Men do all of the time. You're no different.''

Gabriel looked her straight in the eye. "You're wrong, Carly. I'm like no one you've ever dealt with before. I'm your enemy, not your lover. Believe me when I tell you there will come a time when you'll regret ever having met me."

Carly's smile faded. There was something in his voice.... "Are you threatening me?"

"You can take it any way you want to."

As Kate watched the two of them with increasing curiosity, Willa rose from the floor and went to Kate. "Will you color with me?"

Kate reluctantly took her eyes from Gabriel and her sister. "I'm sorry, sweetheart. What did you say?"

"Will you color with me?"

She smiled and touched Willa's cheek. "Of course." She followed her to the table and sat cross-legged beside her on the floor. "What are we working on?"

"You color the little girl in the garden, and I'll color the parrot in the jungle."

Kate checked out the selection of colors, picked out the green crayon and got to work—with occasional curious glances in the direction of Gabriel and Carly.

Gabriel had looked angry, but was now calm. Carly had been smiling, but now looked wary.

Suddenly Gabriel moved away from Carly, set his drink on a table and walked over to his grandmother. "There's someone I have to talk to. I'm afraid I'll miss dinner."

She patted his hand. "All right, dear. Shall I have Mrs. Meredith keep a plate warm for you?"

"I'd appreciate it." Then he walked over to Willa, leaned over and kissed the top of her head. "I'll try to get back before your bedtime. But if I don't make it, I'll read you two stories tomorrow night."

She smiled up at him. "Okay. What do you think of my picture so far?"

"I like your orange jungle," he said as he gave the appearance of seriously studying her artwork. "Green ones are rather boring and predictable."

Willa tilted her head first to one side and then the other as she looked at her work. "That's what I thought."

He looked at Kate's picture as he casually rested his hand on her shoulder. "And you, young lady, need to take some risks. Everybody has red roses. You should color yours blue."

She was so aware of his touch that she could barely hear him over the pounding of her heart.

"Or purple," chimed in Willa.

Focus, thought Kate. Just forget how close he is. "You're right," she managed to say in a voice steadier than she'd expected. Placing the red crayon back into the box, she plucked out both the blue and the purple. "You're both right. I'm too traditional. It's time to break away."

"Good girl," said Gabriel approvingly as he took his hand from her shoulder.

Kate's eyes followed Gabriel as he walked out of the room. She loved looking at him. She could even imag-

ine him as an old man, still tall and straight, and attractive.

But then she felt Carly's eyes on her, so she quickly went back to the coloring book.

Carly sank with a tired-sounding sigh onto the couch across from Kate and Willa. "So," she asked, "how was the carnival?"

Willa smiled, but didn't bother to look up. "We had fun. And after the carnival we went on a picnic."

"I'm sorry you couldn't go with us. What did you do today?" asked Kate, quickly changing the subject.

"I decided to accept a modeling assignment for DeSchoen, so I had to take a commuter flight to London this morning for a fitting."

"I understand that Richard went with you," said Kate as she glanced in his direction and saw that he was flipping quietly through a magazine.

"He had some things to do there."

"I wish you'd told me that's what you were going to do," said Kate. "I would have liked to have come along."

"It was a last-minute thing this morning. You were still sound asleep, and I didn't want to wake you. Especially not after what happened last night."

Laurel Trent looked up from her stitching, her needle poised in midair. "What about last night?"

"Kate had a little accident."

"Almost. Thanks to Gabriel, I didn't."

"What happened?" asked Laurel.

"I'm not sure," said Kate. "Somehow I ended up in the observatory and fell over the railing. Gabriel found

me and managed to pull me back up before I lost my grip."

"How did you fall over the railing?" asked Richard.

"Maybe," suggested Carly, "someone deliberately pushed her."

"Who would do something like that?" asked Laurel, clearly distressed.

"Perhaps a ghost," suggested Richard. "You know, this place—"

"Is rumored to be haunted," Kate finished for him. "I know. It wasn't a ghost."

"But you think someone pushed you?" asked Laurel.

"I did last night, but now I'm not so sure."

"I must admit that I've had some strange things happen to me since moving here," said Carly. "Very strange."

"What kinds of things?" asked Kate.

"Little unexplainable accidents here and there," said Carly mysteriously. "They probably aren't related, though."

"Be more specific."

"My second night here, I was coming down the stairs in the dark, and I could have sworn that someone pushed me. Anyway, I lost my balance, but, as luck would have it, managed to catch myself on the banister before I fell far enough to hurt myself."

"That's a lot like what happened to me in the tower. Did you see anyone?"

"No. I didn't hear anyone, either. Later I decided that I must have tripped. I mean, why would anyone want to harm me?" She cast a glance in Laurel's direction. "Right?"

The older woman quirked an eyebrow at Carly and went back to her stitching without commenting.

"As for you," continued Carly without missing a beat, "who knows what really happened?"

"The more I think about it, the more I believe I was sleepwalking," said Kate. "I must have awakened when I tripped. It's just that it all seemed so real at the time."

"Perhaps the ghosts really were out to get you." She looked at Laurel again. "Maybe they mistook you for me, Katie. I imagine we look identical even to ghosts."

Kate smiled at the ridiculousness of it. "Why would the ghosts want to harm you?"

"Who knows? Perhaps I offended one of them in some way."

"I don't believe in ghosts," said Willa without looking up from her coloring.

"I don't either," said Kate. "And neither does Carly. She was making a joke."

"Don't forget about that car with the blacked-out windows and covered license plate that tried to run you off the road last week," said Richard to Carly.

"What's he talking about?" asked Kate, a worried frown creasing her forehead.

"It's like Richard said. I was driving along, minding my own business, and this other car came along

riding my bumper, went to pass me and tried to edge me off the road.''

"Were either of you able to see who was driving or anything that might identify the car?''

"I wasn't there," said Richard. "My information is strictly secondhand.''

"That's true," said Carly. "I was all alone. I imagine if I'd had anyone with me it wouldn't have happened.''

"Why do you say that?''

Again she looked at the older woman. "Oh, I don't know. It's just a feeling I have.''

Kate wasn't deterred. "Did you call the police?''

"I did about the car incident. They couldn't find anything, of course. The authorities around here are completely incompetent.''

"And don't forget about the shots," said Richard.

"Shots?" asked Kate, now really worried.

"I was out walking and someone shot at me," Carly said matter-of-factly.

Laurel looked at Carly with skeptical eyes. "I personally think it was a car backfiring.''

"Or it might have been hunters," said Richard. "There's a lot of wild game around here.''

"I've never known hunters to be that careless around homes," said Laurel. "It was a car.''

"Did anyone else hear anything?" asked Kate.

"Not that I know of. And yes, I reported that to the police also and they came up with predictably nothing.''

Richard started to say something, but was cut off by Mrs. Meredith, who walked in the door at that moment. "Dinner is ready."

Dinner or no dinner, even as she put the crayons away and rose to follow the others into the dining room, Kate couldn't help but wonder if what had happened to her—if indeed she hadn't been sleepwalking—was connected to what had happened to Carly. Had someone mistaken her for Carly?

But why would anyone want to hurt her sister?

Gabriel Trent had impatiently slammed the knocker on the front door of Harry Granville's home for the third time when Harry himself finally answered.

Gabriel strode quickly past him into the foyer. "I apologize if I'm interrupting anything, Harry, but I can't wait. I need to talk to you right now."

"About what?" asked Harry in surprise as he fell easily into step with Gabriel.

"My charming bride-to-be."

They went into an oak-paneled library that had leather-bound law books, both old and new, lining the walls in dark walnut cases with enclosed glass fronts.

"What's going on?" Harry asked in genuine concern as he waved his friend into a rich-looking burgundy leather chair.

"It has to do with Carly's blackmailing me into this nightmare of a marriage. I think I've figured something out, and it's important that I run it by you."

Harry leaned against the edge of his desk, his hands folded across his chest. "Go ahead."

"I don't think this marriage has anything to do with the fact that Carly is Willa's biological mother."

"What else could it be about?"

"Kate."

"I'm afraid I'm not following you."

"I think that this marriage is nothing more than Carly's way of getting back at her sister."

"For what?"

"I don't know."

"Then what makes you think that?"

"Something Carly said tonight. Listening to her, it sounds as though this whole thing about marriage and instant motherhood is designed to impress Kate."

"Come on, Gabriel. That's a little farfetched. Why would she go to this kind of trouble for something like that?"

"I'm just telling you what it sounds like to me. Something is clearly going on between the two of them. I don't know if Kate's aware of it or not, but it's there."

"What about Willa?"

"She doesn't mean anything to Carly. There's no emotional connection there on either side, and Carly isn't making any attempt to foster one."

"But according to her, she's created this entire marital mess because of Willa."

"So we've been led to believe. I mean, if what Carly said before is to be believed, this marriage is to allow us both to parent Willa in a way that disrupts my daughter's life as little as possible. I didn't believe it the first time she said it to me and I certainly don't believe it now that I've seen her in action."

"All right," said Harry, "be that as it may, how does the change in motive alter the situation? Whatever Carly's reasons, her ability to blackmail you with the loss of Willa remains the same."

"I don't know if it does or not because I don't know what's behind her plotting."

"What's your point?"

"You're not usually so obtuse, Harry. Obviously, if we can figure it out before the wedding, there may be some way to turn this around by reasoning with her."

"I think you're wasting your time."

"Does that mean you won't help me?"

Harry looked at his longtime friend with resigned eyes. "No, of course not. You know I'll help you in any way I can. What exactly is it that you want me to do?"

"Have your investigator check out both sisters and dig up anything he can about them from birth on. If Kate has a part in this, I want to know what it is. And if Carly has a grudge against her sister, I need to know the details. Go to the mother. Talk to their friends. Just do whatever it takes to find out their family secrets. The answer might be in there somewhere. It's my last hope."

"All right. I'll get on it first thing tomorrow."

"Not tomorrow, Harry. I want you on it tonight. We don't have any time to waste."

"Very well. Tonight."

"Thank you, Harry. You're a good friend. Believe me, I appreciate everything you've done to help me."

Harry looked vaguely uneasy as he walked around his desk and sat in his black high-backed chair.

"What's your general impression of the sister now that you've spent some time with her?"

There was a subtle change in Gabriel's expression. "Kate," said Gabriel gently. "It's strange, but I think if she were the one doing the blackmailing, I could learn to live with it."

"She's that different from Carly?"

"There's no comparison, Harry. It's hard to believe they're related, much less twins."

There was an expression in Gabriel's eyes that Harry hadn't seen before. "It could be an act."

"Anything's possible," Gabriel agreed, "but I don't think so. Kate's genuine."

"And you don't think she knows anything?"

"Not about Willa and not about the blackmail."

"What if you were to tell her about the child? If she's as honorable as you seem to think she is, she could cut through the nonsense of guessing, tell you what's going on with her sister and maybe even talk Carly out of what she's doing."

"I can't tell her. Carly threatened to start court proceedings if Kate finds out. I can't take that chance. I'd rather risk the marriage than risk losing Willa to that woman."

"I understand."

"The ball's in your court."

"I'll do what I can."

"Thanks," said Gabriel as he rose and shook Harry's hand. "You're a good friend."

"Yeah," said the lawyer with a half smile, "a good friend who can't seem to get you out of this disaster."

After Gabriel had gone, Harry sank into his chair and rubbed his eyes. He loved Gabriel like a brother. Gabriel and his wife had deeply wanted a child, but Stephanie wasn't able to conceive. They had come to Harry about finding a child and beginning adoption proceedings, and that's exactly what he'd done.

But Harry knew something about Willa's adoption that he'd never told Gabriel.

Now it was coming back to haunt him.

He'd known exactly what kind of woman Carly Fairfax and her mother were when he'd started the adoption proceedings all those years ago. He knew the truth that they were hiding even today.

And he had to sit here helplessly and listen to his friend's distress all because he couldn't tell him Carly's secret. If he did, Harry knew he could lose everything. It didn't matter how pure his motives were at the time. What he'd done was flatly illegal and certainly immoral. Carly had threatened him with the ruin of his years of hard work and his life as he knew it. And she could do it.

He knew—and had known at the time—who Willa's real mother was. And it wasn't Carly.

As he dragged his fingers through his hair, Dee walked in and stood in front of her husband. "I knew from the start that something was wrong with that engagement. Carly Fairfax is nothing like the kind of woman our Gabriel would fall in love with."

"Were you eavesdropping?"

"Yes," she admitted unrepentantly.

"Of all the conversations for you to overhear," he said tiredly. "Dee, you have to forget it."

"Not a chance, my love. You and I are going to put a stop to this sham."

"We can't."

"Of course we can. We'll whisk Willa away someplace where Carly can't find her."

"Then Gabriel will end up in jail charged with kidnapping. Is that what you want, Dee?"

"Well, no, but...."

"Our hands are tied. There's nothing we can do. And you, my dear, are going to have to keep your well-intended mouth shut. What you overheard can't leave this room. Not ever."

"But if Kate Fairfax can help..."

"She can't help, Dee. And above all, she can never, ever know about Willa."

"You mean she mustn't know that Willa is really Carly's daughter?"

Harry's gaze shifted to the floor. "Yes."

"And what if I think that both you and Gabriel are making a terrible mistake in not telling her?"

"As much as I love you, Dee, and you know I do, I'd have to tell you that it's none of your business. Willa is Gabriel's daughter and this is his call all of the way."

Dee put her arms around her husband of fifteen years and hugged him tightly.

Men, she thought with resignation. They somehow managed to make simple things complicated and, contrary to their opinions of themselves, had absolutely no intuition when it came to predicting women's behav-

ior. Or anyone's behavior, for that matter. The woman she'd met in her home would never do anything to jeopardize Gabriel's custody of Willa, regardless of whether or not her sister was the child's mother. Kate was clearly, in Dee's opinion, the kind of woman who would want what was best for the child.

On the other hand, Dee had disliked Carly from the moment she'd met her. There was a blankness behind her eyes as though something was missing; an emptiness in her smile. The camera loved her, but the camera lied.

Dee could and would fix this. Her husband and Gabriel might be angry for a time, but they would eventually realize that she was right about this and thank her for interfering.

If not, she'd face the consequences when they happened.

Chapter Ten

While Gabriel was still at Harry's, Kate was busy pushing the food around her plate rather than eating it.

Carly watched her curiously for a few minutes. "Kate? Do you feel all right?"

Kate managed a small smile. Nothing had happened between her and Gabriel, but that didn't stop her guilty thoughts from gnawing at her. "Yes. I guess I'm not very hungry."

"Probably because of your late picnic."

Willa drained the last of her milk from the glass and set it on the table with a thunk. "May I please be excused, Nana?"

"Of course, dear. It's time for you to get ready for bed. You have school tomorrow."

Willa walked to Kate and leaned against her chair. "Will you read to me again tonight, Kate?"

"I'd love to, but maybe you'd prefer it if Carly read to you. She's a wonderful storyteller."

Willa turned toward Carly with a noticeable lack of enthusiasm. "Would you?" she asked politely.

Carly didn't even bother looking at the little girl. "Not tonight. I have too much to do."

"Carly," said Kate, "it'll just take a few minutes."

"Not tonight," she said more firmly.

As Willa rose, Richard got up, lifted her high in his arms and tossed her over his shoulder. "I'll go upstairs with you, beautiful, but I can't hang around too long. I have plans."

Willa laughed delightedly. "Uncle Richard, you're silly."

"So you women keep telling me."

The little girl waved at Kate over Richard's shoulder as they disappeared through the doorway.

Laurel delicately dabbed her mouth with her napkin and rose. "If you'll excuse me, ladies. One of my favorite television programs is on. I never miss it."

"And then there were two," said Carly when she'd gone. "The one bad thing about this place is that there always seems to be someone around."

"I should think that would be one of its charms." Kate placed her napkin neatly beside her plate. "I'd like to talk to you."

"About?"

"Lots of things. We haven't seen each other for more than a year, and it's been nearly impossible to spend time with you since I arrived in England."

"I know," agreed Carly. "It's just that I've been so busy. You know how weddings are."

"Are you sure that's what it is, Carly? I've had the feeling you're avoiding me."

"Why would I do that? I'm the one who asked you to come here in the first place."

"I know. It's just a feeling I'm getting."

"I'm sorry. I'll try to do better at organizing my time so that we're together more."

Kate cleared her throat as she got ready to say what was really on her mind. She'd been thinking about it ever since the picnic that afternoon. "Actually, Carly, I've been thinking that it might be better if I were to return home until it's closer to your actual wedding date. I don't seem to be very useful."

"Don't be silly," said Carly. "I want you here now. I need you with me for this."

"No, you don't. It's obvious that you have things very much under control."

Carly leaned back in her chair and eyed her sister. "What's going on here? You and I both know that you hate to fly. Why would you want to go all the way back to Chicago, only to have to turn around and come back?"

"So that you can do what you have to do without worrying about entertaining me."

Carly laughed. "Don't take this the wrong way, Katie, but I don't give so much as a thought to your

entertainment. I know you can take care of yourself for a few days. But I need you here with me now. You're the only family I have.''

"There's Mom."

"She doesn't count."

"She's going to be crushed when she finds out you're getting married and didn't invite her."

"That's not my problem," said Carly coldly.

"What happened between the two of you? You used to be so close. Now she won't mention your name and you won't invite her to your wedding."

"Katie, you know as well as I do that woman wouldn't get on a plane to come here even if I were to invite her. Certainly not for my wedding."

"Still, you could make an effort. She's not young anymore. I think if you try to meet her halfway..."

"You apparently haven't figured this out yet, but the woman is bad news. If you want to keep her in your life, that's your business, but don't force her onto me."

"She's never done anything to either one of us except try to raise us the best she could on her own. I know she made some mistakes, but so have the two of us over the years."

Carly looked at Kate in genuine astonishment. "You are completely clueless. You take everyone at face value without bothering to consider what their ulterior motives might be."

"This is our mother we're talking about. What ulterior motives could she have had for anything she's done except for our welfare?"

"I'm almost looking forward to your finding out, just to see your reaction. And you will. Soon." She thought about what she'd said and smiled. "Very soon, I think."

"Find out what?"

"That, my dear twin, is for another time. Before the wedding, I think. You won't have to wait much longer."

Kate didn't believe a word of what her sister was saying. This was just Carly acting out. She'd learned as a child that she had to accept Carly the way she was or let her go altogether. And letting her twin go wasn't something Kate was willing to do.

Carly picked up her glass of wine and took a long sip as she eyed Kate over the rim. "Anyway, back to the entertainment factor. If you're bored, all you have to do is look around you. This house might not be to my taste, but it's interesting. It looks like something you and Jane would have created out of cardboard when we were little."

"I know," said Kate with a reminiscent smile. "I think it's beautiful. And it has so many interesting nooks and crannies. Jane would love it."

"Good old Jane," said Carly without enthusiasm. "What's she up to these days?"

"Still running her bookstore."

"Do you see her very often?"

"A few times a week. We usually have lunch together."

"Is she still single?" Carly asked the question as though being single were a bad thing.

"Happily so. She likes being on her own."

"It's not like she has a choice. She's never been able to keep a man interested."

Kate smiled. More vintage Carly. "I think it's been the other way around."

"You still protect her."

"There's nothing to protect. Jane is her own person. That's what I loved about her when we were children and that's what I love about her now."

Carly leaned back in her chair and played with her unused salad fork. "You probably aren't aware of this, but I used to envy your friendship with her."

"Why would you? Jane was your friend, too."

"It wasn't the same. It was almost as though the two of you were the twins."

Kate had to admit she was right. If she could have picked a sister, it would have been Jane. "You had your own group of friends."

Carly nodded. "True enough. We went through some rough times, didn't we?"

"That's for sure."

"Do you still think about your baby?"

Kate looked down at her lap and suddenly had trouble swallowing. "Yes."

"It's been a long time. I should think you'd be over it by now."

"I don't imagine one ever gets over the death of a child."

"But you never even saw her."

Kate raised her eyes to Carly's. "I gave birth to her. And I think about her every day of my life. Every single day."

Carly chose her next words with great deliberation and watched Kate carefully for her reaction. "I suppose looking at Willa must be like seeing a ghost. She looks exactly the way your daughter would probably look today if she'd lived."

"Yes," said Kate, her voice catching ever so slightly, "she certainly does."

"Well, that's water under the bridge. When you finally meet the right man, you'll have a whole houseful of babies that look like Willa."

"I'll never have another child."

"Why not?"

"I couldn't bear to lose another baby. I won't risk it."

"You'll change your mind."

"Never." She changed the subject away from herself. "What about you and Gabriel? Are you planning a large family?"

"Not right away. I don't want to do anything at this point in my career to mess up my figure."

"There are other models with children and healthy careers."

"Some. Not many."

"Well, at least you'll have Willa. She's a sweetheart."

"If you say so," said Carly unenthusiastically.

"I do. She has a very loving nature. You should take some time to get to know her before the wedding, and to let her get to know you."

"She doesn't want me to marry her father, you know."

"Of course she doesn't. No child wants to share her father with a stranger. But once the three of you are a family and she realizes that you only add to her happiness rather than take away from it, everything will be fine."

"I don't know...."

"Give her some time to adjust."

"Okay. Whatever."

Kate sipped her wine and studied her sister.

Carly looked back at her. "Now that you've spent some time with Gabriel, what do you think of him?"

"He's wonderful."

Carly smiled. "I agree."

"You're a very lucky woman."

"Jealous?"

"You know better than that. I'm happy for you. I always knew you'd find the perfect man someday."

Carly leaned back and watched her sister with the tiniest of smiles curving her mouth.

"What?"

"Nothing. I'm just enjoying the moment. Have you dated anyone seriously since Jeff?"

"No," said Kate quietly.

"Don't you think it's about time?"

"I'm not looking. If the right man happens my way, great. If not, that's all right, too. I have a good life."

Carly suddenly looked at her watch. "Oh, God, I didn't realize it was so late. I have to take off."

"Where are you going?"

"Out."

"Carly..."

"Don't look at me like that. I'm not doing anything wrong. But I need for you to do a favor for me."

"What?"

"I'll be leaving with Richard in about fifteen minutes. After that, if you see Gabriel around, pretend you're me."

Kate shook her head. "Oh, no. Not a chance."

"Please, Katie? I need to tell Richard that whatever we had in the past is over. And I can't do it here."

"I don't know...."

"Please? Just do this one little favor for me."

Kate relented. She'd just stay in her room and avoid seeing Gabriel altogether. Then there wouldn't be a problem. "All right."

"Thank you!" As she rose from the table, she leaned over and caught Kate's face between her hands. "I have a feeling," she said, "that one day soon you're going to get exactly what you deserve." She kissed Kate squarely on the forehead. "I know we've had our troubles in the past, but believe me when I tell you that I'm happy you're here. So don't take off on me, okay? Stay until after the wedding. That's not too much for one sister to ask another, is it?"

"Of course not. I'll stay."

"Good." Carly straightened away from her. "I promise that tomorrow we'll do something together."

She looked at her watch again. "Gotta go. Richard's waiting."

And then there was one, thought Kate.

She pushed her chair back and rose, then headed for the staircase and Willa's room.

She heard a man's voice coming from inside and thought that perhaps Richard was still with Willa.

When she tapped on the door and opened it, she found Gabriel sitting on the edge of the bed reading a story.

"Oh, I'm sorry," she said as she backed out. "I didn't mean to intrude."

Willa sat upright. "Please don't go, Kate. You promised you'd read to me, too."

Gabriel's eyes met Kate's as he held out the book. "You do the second half."

Kate reluctantly walked toward the bed and sat on the opposite side from Gabriel. She was completely aware of the man. And when his fingers brushed against hers as he handed her the book, it was like a shock of electricity rolling through her body.

"Where did you leave off?" she asked as evenly as she could manage, forcing down her reaction to him.

"He wants to move to Australia," said Willa helpfully as she pointed at the page.

"Here we are," said Kate as she found the place, and launched herself into the telling of the story.

Kate could feel Gabriel watching her, and wished he would stop. At one point, she looked up from the book to let him see her impatience, but it didn't do any good. He continued to gaze at her.

Gabriel wasn't staring with the intention of upsetting Kate. It was just that she was the kind of woman it was hard to look away from. Her voice was naturally a little husky, and soothing. It was an interesting voice. Sexy. And he liked watching her different expressions as she read, as though she couldn't help putting herself into the shoes of the various characters.

He loved looking at her.

When Kate finished, she closed the book and smiled at Willa. "If I don't see you in the morning before you go to school, have a wonderful day."

"I will."

She leaned over and kissed her on the forehead. "Good night, sweetheart."

"'Night, Kate."

Kate rose from the bed and left the room to walk hurriedly to her own. More than anything at that moment, she didn't want to have another encounter with Gabriel.

"Kate?"

His voice called her from down the hall.

Kate, walking faster, acted as though she hadn't heard him and reached for her door handle.

But he caught up to her, and she felt Gabriel put his hand over hers. "What's wrong?"

Kate stood with her back to him, his hand still on hers. "I'd like to go to my room."

"Not until you tell me what's wrong."

She still didn't turn. "You know the answer to that perfectly well and you're not helping any."

"Ah," he said, "you're attracted to your sister's fiancé. Is that the problem?"

Now Kate turned and looked directly at him. "If I am attracted to you, it's not a problem because I don't plan on acting on it."

"What if you were to discover that your sister's fiancé is also attracted to you?"

"Don't say that."

"It hits me broadside every time I look at you."

"That's because when you look at me, you see Carly."

He shook his head. "No. Not after our first encounter."

His eyes moved over her face. Gabriel had to admit that he didn't understand what he was feeling. This was the twin sister of the woman who was making his life a living hell and threatening his only child. And all he could think about doing was pulling her into his arms and kissing her until neither of them could think straight.

"I wish," he said quietly, "that we could have met under different circumstances."

Her eyes met his. "But we didn't. I think we should spend as little time in each other's company as possible between now and the wedding."

"That won't change anything."

"Please leave me alone. I just want to get through the wedding and get out of here."

"You don't need to be afraid of me."

Kate smiled halfheartedly. "Yes, well, sometimes there's no accounting for my emotions. If you'll ex-

cuse me,'' she said as she turned away from him to open her door. "I'm going to go to bed now."

Without saying anything else, Gabriel walked away from her.

Kate, her heart hammering, watched until he rounded the corner. Then she slowly turned, went into her room and closed the door behind her.

She was just going to have to stay away from him.

Kate, still in her clothes, was lying on top of her covers reading a book. She glanced at the clock and saw that it was midnight. Time to go to sleep.

She had just gotten up when she heard a knock. It wasn't on her door. Maybe it was Carly's.

She crossed the room, opened her door and looked down the hall. Gabriel stood in front of Carly's door. He saw her before she could duck back in.

"Do you know where she is?" asked Gabriel.

Kate didn't know what to say.

"Kate?" he asked, walking toward her.

Kate left her room completely and closed the door behind her. "I'm Carly," she said.

Gabriel looked her up and down. "Why are you wearing the same thing Kate had on earlier?"

Kate couldn't help the tint that came to her cheeks. She'd never been a very good liar. "We're twins, so we exchange clothes."

"I see." And Gabriel did see. All too well.

He stepped toward her.

Kate backed up.

He took another step.

Kate's back hit the wall.

Gabriel put one hand on the wall above her shoulder and raised his other hand to her face, gently stroking her cheek. "We need to spend more time alone," he said, leaning toward her and nuzzling her ear.

"I'm a little busy right now," said Kate in a failed attempt at matter-of-factness.

Gabriel kissed her earlobe and gently tugged on it with his teeth. "Too busy for this?"

Kate could feel his warm breath, could hear it. "Well, I . . . I . . ."

"Shh," he whispered as he lifted her heavy hair, kissed the tender spot just behind her ear and began caressing the side of her neck with his lips.

Kate thought her legs were going to buckle beneath her. Gabriel, however, eliminated that possibility when he put his arm around her waist and pulled her body close to his. Her own body stiffened in response.

His lips moved over the line of her jaw to the corner of her mouth.

"Should we be doing this in the hall? What if someone sees us?"

"We're engaged."

"It's just that I . . ."

"You're talking way too much," said Gabriel as he raised his head and looked into her eyes. "I guess there's only one way to silence you."

Kate's heart flew into her throat as he lowered his lips to hers. She tried desperately not to respond. It didn't matter that he thought she was Carly. Kate knew

perfectly well who she was, and she had no business in this man's arms.

Gabriel wouldn't let her get away with no response. He coaxed her lips apart and began exploring, gently at first and then more deeply, more intimately.

Kate melted from the inside out. Her body started doing naturally what her mind told it not to. She began to kiss him back, tangling her fingers in his thick hair. Gabriel's hands moved over her hips and pulled her more tightly against him so that she could feel how much he wanted her.

She couldn't think. Didn't want to. All Kate knew was that she'd never been kissed like this before and she wanted this man desperately.

Gabriel raised his head and looked into her eyes. Both of them were out of breath.

He kissed her again, more harshly than before, then stepped away from her. He let his eyes slowly wander over her, starting with her lips, lingering on her softly rounded breasts and hips, then down her long legs and up again, stopping at her eyes.

Kate stood there in all of her clothes feeling suddenly very, very naked and vulnerable.

"Do me a favor," he said with a quiet anger that was far more chilling than a display of temper. "When Carly comes back, tell her I want to see her."

The color drained from Kate's face. "What makes you think...?"

"You're a terrible liar, Kate. Perhaps you should take some lessons from your sister."

"How did you know?"

"I just did."

Kate leaned her head against the wall and closed her eyes. What kind of woman was she that she could respond like that to her sister's fiancé? Despite the cold water Gabriel had thrown, her body still tingled from his touch.

And suddenly his arms were around her again, holding her tightly. "God, I can't be angry with you."

Kate pressed her hand against his chest. "Don't."

"Don't what? Don't want you? Can you stop yourself from wanting me?"

"No," she whispered.

Gabriel looked into her eyes for a long moment. Kate could see his feelings so clearly. This man she'd thought so cold at first.

She reached out her hand and touched his face. He could see tears welling in her eyes. "If you feel for me what I see in your eyes," she said, "don't put me in this position. I can't betray my sister, but I'm running out of strength to stay away from you. Please don't do this to me."

Gabriel covered her hand with his. He drew her palm from his cheek to his lips and kissed it with a lingering gentleness.

Then he turned and walked away.

"Oh, Kate," she whispered to no one, "what have you done?"

Chapter Eleven

Kate tossed and turned all night. She must have slept some, because she'd open her eyes to look at the clock and see that an hour had passed. She couldn't stop thinking about Gabriel.

When she gave up trying to sleep any longer, she slipped out of her nightgown, letting it fall around her feet in a soft cotton cloud, then stepped into the shower, face first into a spray of warm water. She let it wash over her hair and run down her body in rivulets, slowly turning until her back was to the spray.

For a long time, Kate just stood there enjoying the steamy warmth before she lathered up her hair and body. Turning under the spray, she let the clean water rinse the suds away.

As she stepped out of the shower, Kate toweled herself off, then wiped the steam from the mirror and took a long, hard look at herself. She had to stay away from Gabriel. Far, far away.

Kate turned away from the mirror while she finished toweling off her hair. Back in the bedroom, she struggled into another pair of Carly's jeans, sucking in her stomach as far as she could to close the button. Pulling up the zipper nearly cost her three fingernails. And when she was finally sealed into them, there was no way she was going to unseal herself to attempt to tuck in a shirt—even if she'd had one long enough to need it. Instead, she pulled out one of two T-shirts left in Carly's bag. Like yesterday's, it left her midriff bare. She could only hope her suitcases had been located by now.

It wasn't even seven o'clock when she left her room and went next door to Carly's. She tapped lightly on the door. When there was no answer—and she hadn't really been expecting one—she opened the door a crack to see if Carly was there.

She was. Kate could make out her shape under the bedcovers in the dimly lit room. She quietly closed the door and went downstairs, passing and greeting an expressionless Mrs. Peabody along the way. She inclined her head but didn't speak.

The delicious smell of bacon led her to the kitchen. Mrs. Meredith smiled at Kate as she walked in. "Hungry this morning?"

"Starving!"

"Go ahead and take some toast. The rest will be ready in a few minutes."

Kate lifted a corner of toast from a buttered stack on a covered plate and took a big bite out of it.

The cook watched her with a smile. "Take another one if you want."

Kate did. "Thanks. If I eat too much, though, you'd better run for cover. When the button on these jeans finally goes, there could be casualties."

"Are they your sister's?"

"Yes. I'd have to live on rice cakes for a year to fit into them properly."

"You look fine. Men like curves on a woman, despite what the magazines tell us."

"What I'd like are some clothes that fit. Is there a telephone and directory I could use?"

"Is it a private conversation?"

"No. I just want to call the airport to see if they've found my luggage."

"Then you can use the one over there." She aimed her wooden spoon at the far end of the kitchen where there was a white wall phone. "The directory is in the drawer just beneath it."

"Thanks." Still munching on her toast, Kate pulled out the directory with one hand and thumbed through the pages until she found the number of the airport. After popping the last bite into her mouth, she delicately wiped the tips of her fingers on her jeans and dialed.

No luck. Her luggage was still lost. Kate hung up with a sigh. "I have to buy some clothes. Is there a shop nearby?"

"Not really what you'd call nearby, although I suppose that depends on how you get there."

"What do you mean?"

"If you drive, it's about an hour away. If you take the launch, it's just across the way, perhaps ten minutes."

"The launch is easier," said Gabriel from the open doorway, "but with your aversion to water, I think you should stick to land and leave your sister to the launch."

Kate's heart leapt at the sight of him. He was wearing wire-rimmed glasses, and she was struck by the fact that he was, if possible, even better-looking with them. "Does Carly use it?"

"All of the time." He walked farther into the kitchen and took a slice of toast. "If you need to go somewhere, I can take you in the car."

"No!"

He lifted a dark eyebrow.

"I mean, no, thank you," she said more gently. "I don't want to be a bother."

"You're not, Kate. Not at all." His eyes caught and held hers.

The cook, still stirring, glanced from one to the other. She wasn't exactly sure what she was looking at, but it was definitely something interesting.

"Just the same, I think I'll wait for Carly and drive into town with her."

"Breakfast is ready," said the cook. "Where's Willa?"

"I just checked on her," said Gabriel. "She'll be down in a minute or two."

"Then take your places in the breakfast room so you can eat while it's still warm."

"Breakfast room?" asked Kate.

"Turn left out of the kitchen. You'll find it."

Kate had to walk past Gabriel to get through the doorway. Her arm barely brushed against him, but even that slight contact sent her pulse soaring.

And his. Gabriel watched the very appealing and unconsciously sexy swing of her hips as she walked away from him. Looking away didn't help. The air around him held the delicate scent of her perfume.

Kate, unaware of the scrutiny, walked down the wide hallway to the end, and right there, in a semicircle of floor-to-ceiling paned windows was a tiled area with a round table at its center. The room looked like sunshine, it was so cheery and bright, with large plants strategically placed to catch the sun. Laurel Trent was already seated and reading a newspaper with a cup of coffee raised halfway to her lips.

"Good morning," said Kate, the relief that she wasn't having breakfast alone with Gabriel evident in her face.

The older woman smiled at her in surprise. "I thought you'd be sleeping in this morning."

Kate wasn't sure where to sit. Gabriel pulled out the chair next to his grandmother and waved her into it.

As Kate sat down, she did her best to ignore Gabriel. Taking the lemon yellow cloth napkin from beside her plate, Kate put it on her lap. "Thank you," she said without looking at him and then continued speaking to his grandmother. "I haven't been able to sleep very well since I arrived here."

Laurel nodded. "New bed. New surroundings. And the sea can seem very loud when you're not used to it." Her face suddenly lit up as she saw Willa skip in, dressed in a pleated plaid jumper and turtleneck sweater. "Good morning, darling. Come give your nana a kiss."

Willa dutifully planted a peck on the offered cheek, then tugged on Kate to lean down so she could kiss her, too.

Kate touched Willa's soft, childishly rounded cheek and smiled at her with a warmth that came from her heart. "Good morning."

"Does my hair look shinier today?"

Kate appeared to give her question serious consideration. "I think it just might."

"I'm going to keep brushing it the way you showed me." She scooted onto her chair and waited politely while Gabriel put scrambled eggs, bacon and toast on her plate, then she put her napkin on her lap and began to eat. Kate thought she was like a miniature grown-up—except she swung her legs back and forth under her seat as she ate.

"What are you going to do in school today?" asked Gabriel.

"Jamie's bringing his dog and her new puppies for us to see." She looked at her father sideways and seemed to be thinking about the right way to say something. "His mom says they have to find new homes for the puppies."

To Kate's amazement, Gabriel's eyes lit with quiet amusement. "And?" he asked.

Willa did her best to act casual. "Do you remember what the fortune-teller said about my getting a dog?"

"Yes."

"Well, I was wondering if maybe I could have one of Jamie's." Now she looked her dad straight in the eye. "I promise I'll take care of it myself and it won't be any trouble. Honestly."

"Why don't you wait until after you've seen them, then we'll talk some more about it."

Willa beamed. "Thank you."

"I didn't say you could have one. Not yet, at least." She still smiled.

"You better hurry, honey," said Gabriel as he looked at his watch. "Your bus will be here in a few minutes."

Willa wiped her mouth with her napkin and started to get up.

"Drink your juice first," said Gabriel.

Willa dutifully drained the glass.

"Where's your book bag?"

"In the hall."

"Okay. I'll walk you out. Excuse me, ladies," he said as he rose from the table.

Willa slipped her hand into her father's as they walked to the door. Then Willa turned around and looked at Kate. "Will you be here when I get home?"

"I'm not sure. It depends on my sister."

"Oh," she said sadly.

"What time do you usually get home?"

"Two-thirty."

"Then I'll try very hard to be here."

Willa beamed at her.

Gabriel watched Kate as she looked at his daughter. Willa was clearly crazy about the woman. And Kate? There was a tenderness in her expression when she looked at his daughter. A warmth. Kate clearly felt connected to Willa, but did she sense the reason?

He gently tugged Willa's hand. "Come on."

"The child has taken quite a liking to you," said Laurel as she continued with her breakfast.

"And I to her," said Kate.

"I hope your sister can work the same magic."

Kate moved the eggs around her plate with her fork. "I'm sure when the rush of planning the wedding has subsided, she'll take the time to get to know Willa."

"Hmm."

"Everything has apparently happened so quickly."

"Indeed. It's taken everyone by surprise." She glanced at Kate to gauge her reaction. "Including you, I imagine."

"Especially me. When she sent the telegram to say she needed me to come here right away, she didn't mention anything about a wedding. I assumed she was in trouble."

"Why would you have assumed that? Does Carly get into trouble often?"

Kate glanced up from her eggs. "I didn't mean to imply that. It's just that she wasn't clear about what was going on, and I apparently mistook her excitement for something else."

"You still seem troubled by something."

Kate smiled uneasily. "I don't know why."

"Is it Gabriel?"

Kate looked at the older woman. "Why would you think that?"

"There seems to be a certain tension between the two of you."

"Oh."

"You'll discover as you get to know my grandson that he's a very controlled man. Even I never know what he's feeling or thinking."

"What was his first wife like?"

Laurel smiled. "She was a beautiful girl. She and Gabriel had known each other since childhood. They were the very best of friends. I know he still misses her."

"That's nice. I'd like to have someone like that to marry."

"It has its pros and cons. You see, while they were dear friends, there was no spark between them. They were comfortable with each other. Too comfortable. There were no arguments, no making up." She delicately lifted her shoulders. "No passion, I'm afraid."

"I like being comfortable with a man."

"You'd like it until you met the man of your dreams. Then your sought-after comfort would seem like a prison."

"Maybe. Anyway, I've pretty much given up on meeting the man of my dreams. He doesn't exist."

"Of course he does. You just haven't met him yet. Or if you have met him, you haven't recognized him. You're far too young to have given up on love."

"I might look young on the outside, but there are times when I feel very, very old."

"Never say the word 'old' when you're speaking to a woman in her eighties."

Kate smiled.

Laurel took the napkin from her lap and placed it on the table as she rose. "What are you going to do with your morning?"

"I don't know. Wait for Carly to wake up, I suppose."

"That sounds exciting," she said wryly. "I have some errands to run. I'll see you this afternoon."

Kate stayed in her seat for a few minutes after Laurel had gone. She loved this room. It was the perfect place to start the day. She imagined it would seem cheery even on gloomy days.

Gabriel came back into the room. "Where's my grandmother?"

After her heart did its initial lurch, Kate put on a smile as she rose. "She said she had some errands to run. Did Willa get off to school all right?"

"Yes."

"It was nice that you were able to have breakfast with her."

"I have breakfast with my daughter every morning."

Kate nervously shifted her weight from one foot to the other. "I think I'll see if Carly's awake."

"She won't be. She apparently sleeps past noon unless she's working."

"Then I have things to do on my own."

"Such as?"

Kate's mind was completely blank. She suddenly couldn't think of a thing she had to do.

"Don't avoid me, Kate."

Her eyes met his, too surprised to dissemble. "I have to."

"We're going to be living under the same roof for the next week. It's inevitable that we'll see each other. Often."

"Then we'll deal with it. But we don't have to have conversations, particularly when no one else is around."

"You're behaving as though we've done something wrong."

"What do you call what happened last night?"

"An object lesson. Don't lie to me again, Kate."

"I'm sorry. I wish I hadn't."

His eyes moved over her lovely face feature by feature. He wanted to touch her. His hand clenched into a fist.

"Excuse me," said Kate as she started to move past him, but Gabriel caught her arm. She pulled it away

and turned to face him. "Please," she said, her voice almost a whisper as she looked pleadingly into his eyes. "I won't do this to my sister."

Gabriel said nothing, but his eyes spoke volumes.

Kate felt her knees weaken. "Don't," she said.

"Don't what?" he asked.

"Look at me—like that."

The muscle in his jaw moved. He started to raise his hand to her face.

Panic filled Kate's eyes.

Gabriel saw it and immediately backed off. "It's all right," he said gently. "Relax. I won't do anything to compromise you." He turned away from her and left the room.

Kate closed her eyes and put her hand over her pounding heart. That was it. The moment the wedding was over, she was going to go back to the safety of Chicago.

Straightening her shoulders, she was about to leave the breakfast room when Mrs. Peabody came down the hallway straight toward her. Kate groaned inwardly.

"Excuse me, Miss Fairfax, but you have a—"

Before she could finish her sentence, Dee Granville walked up quickly behind her. "Thank you, Mrs. Peabody. You may leave now. I need to speak with Kate alone."

Kate looked at Dee in surprise. "You want to talk to me?"

Dee took Kate by the hand and pulled her to the window seat that ran along one curved wall. "Sit, sit,"

she said impatiently as she lowered herself onto the cushion.

"What's going on?" asked Kate as she sank beside her.

Dee looked at Kate, then rose and paced the room.

Kate waited, wondering what on earth was wrong.

Finally Dee sat beside her again. "Look," she said, "I don't know you and you don't know me. I'm in a situation right now, though, where I'm going to have to trust you. I hope I can."

Now Kate was really worried. "What is it?"

"It's about your sister and Gabriel."

"Yes?"

Dee paused as she looked out the window. "God, I hope I'm doing the right thing."

Kate looked as confused as she felt.

"Before I say anything, I want you to know that if my husband finds out I've told you any of this, he's going to be very, very angry. You mustn't tell anyone the source of your information. May I have your word?"

"Of course."

"Ordinarily I wouldn't even meddle, but I love Gabriel so dearly. And you obviously love your sister, and I'm sure want the best for her."

"You're beginning to frighten me."

"I don't mean to, but this is an ugly business."

Kate waited.

Dee exhaled a long breath. "I overheard a conversation between Gabriel and my husband last night. It

seems that your sister is blackmailing Gabriel into marrying her."

"Blackmailing?" Kate needed to say the word aloud to comprehend it. "That's ridiculous. Carly wouldn't do something like that."

"I'm telling you what I heard."

"Blackmailing him over what?"

"Willa."

"You're not making sense."

Dee looked at her with apologetic eyes. "I'm so sorry if what I'm about to say is shocking to you. Gabriel and my husband clearly believe you don't know."

"Know what?"

"That Carly is Willa's real mother."

Kate was speechless. All she could do was stare at Dee.

"Are you all right?"

"That's not possible," said Kate when she'd recovered her voice. "Carly has never had a child."

"My husband checked her claim out very thoroughly, as you can imagine. Willa is definitely her child. She apparently found out that Gabriel adopted her and now she's threatening him with the loss of Willa's custody unless he marries her."

Kate was still trying to take in the fact that her sister had a child and had never breathed a word of it to her. "She would have told me."

"She didn't, Kate."

She focused on the woman across from her. "You said she's blackmailing Gabriel into marriage?"

"Exactly. If he doesn't marry her, she's going to take him to court to get custody of Willa."

Kate shook her head. "You have to be wrong. Carly would never do such a thing."

"Believe me, she's doing it. And you have to stop her."

Kate rose and walked to the other side of the breakfast room. "Who is Willa's father?"

"I don't know."

"It's not Gabriel?"

"Good heavens no."

It had to be Jeff. Willa was six. That would have made Carly pregnant at almost the same time Kate herself had been. That meant she'd been telling the truth about Jeff, and Jeff was Willa's father.

Kate felt as though she was going to be ill, and it showed in the sudden pallor of her face.

"Are you all right?" asked Dee.

"Yes," said Kate softly, and then more strongly, "Yes."

"You have to talk your sister out of this marriage."

Kate turned to face Dee. "You're sure this marriage is based on blackmail?"

"I heard it straight from Gabriel's mouth and when I brought it up to my husband, he acknowledged it."

That would certainly explain Gabriel's behavior.

"Kate, she's ruining lives. You must convince her that it's in Willa's best interest to be left with the only father she's ever known."

"I've never been able to talk Carly out of anything."

"But you'll try?"

"Of course I will." Kate rubbed her forehead.

Dee crossed the room to Kate and lightly touched her shoulder. "I'm so sorry to drop this on you in such a sudden fashion. I can only imagine what kind of shock this must be for you. Believe me when I tell you that I appreciate your help and your discretion about my part in whatever happens next."

"Don't worry, Dee. I won't say anything about you."

"Thank you."

At that moment, Gabriel walked back into the room.

Dee flashed him a nervous smile. "Good morning, Gabriel."

"Dee. What are you doing here so early?"

She quickly turned to pick up her purse from the window seat and slung it over her shoulder. "I was unsuccessfully trying to talk Kate into going out to lunch with me later."

Kate couldn't deal with small talk. She certainly couldn't look at Gabriel, knowing what her sister was doing. "Excuse me," she said tightly as she walked past both Gabriel and Dee.

Gabriel's surprised eyes followed her.

Dee deflected his attention by grabbing his arm and tugging on it. "Walk me to my car."

When Kate got to her sister's room, she stopped in front of the door. Three times her hand hovered over the handle, and three times it fell to her side.

She had no idea what to say.

Again her hand touched the cool metal. This time she pushed it down. The door opened. She went straight to the bed. "Carly," she said, shaking her sister's shoulder. "Carly, wake up."

Carly, who was lying on her stomach, pulled a pillow over her head. "Go away, Kate."

Kate took away the pillow. "You might as well talk to me. I'm not leaving until you do."

"What time is it?"

"I don't know. Eight. Eight-thirty."

"In the morning?"

"That's right."

"I've only had three hours of sleep. We'll talk later."

Kate went to the windows and pulled open the drapes to let daylight flood the room. "Now."

Carly let out a huge sigh. With obvious reluctance, she rolled onto her back. "What is so important that it can't wait?"

Kate sat on the edge of the bed. "I want you to tell me the truth about you and Gabriel."

Carly's expression went from annoyed to suspicious. "What do you mean?"

"Why are you really getting married?"

"For the same reason most people get married, Kate. We're in love with each other."

"I don't think so."

"Why else would we be doing it?"

"You tell me."

"This is ridiculous. I don't have to explain myself or my life to you, and certainly not my choice of a husband."

"I'm not sitting in judgment, Carly. I just want you to tell me the truth."

Carly raised herself up on her elbows. "Did Gabriel say something to you?"

"Like what?"

"Just something."

Kate watched her closely. "No."

"Then what are you talking about?"

Kate couldn't say it. She settled for "You don't act like a couple in love." That, also, was true.

With a sigh, Carly sat up, stacked some pillows behind her and leaned against them. "All right, Kate. You want to know what's going on, I'll tell you. Gabriel has been getting a lot of flak from his family and friends about marrying me. You must have noticed that no one here is exactly thrilled at the prospect of having me in the family. And it's beginning to have an effect on our relationship."

Kate sighed inwardly. She had hoped for the truth, but forged ahead anyway. "Why would they not want him to marry you?"

"Who knows? Maybe it's because I'm a model. Maybe they're jealous. Maybe they just can't see him with anyone but his dead wife." She shrugged. "Whatever it is, they're chipping away at us."

"That's all there is to it?"

"That's it."

Kate gazed at her sister and realized that she didn't know her at all. She tried a different approach. "Carly, are you sure Gabriel is the man you want to marry?"

"Absolutely."

"Because you love him?"

"That's right."

"And he loves you the way you deserve to be loved?"

"Does anyone ever get loved the way they deserve to be?" A corner of her mouth lifted in a cynical smile. "Look who I'm asking? The eternal virgin. Except, of course, for that one little tumble down Mount Olympus with Jeff seven years ago. Did Jeff love you the way you deserved, Katie?"

"This isn't about Jeff and me. It's about Gabriel and you." She paused. "And Willa."

Again Carly eyed her as though trying to figure out how much she knew. "What does she have to do with anything?"

Kate jumped in with both feet. "Is Willa your daughter, Carly? Are you making Gabriel marry you with a threat that you'll take Willa away from him if he doesn't?"

"That's ridiculous!"

"Is it?" Kate looked at her sister with sad eyes, but Carly was unfazed.

"Is there more of this inquisition, or can I get back to sleep?"

Kate rose from the bed. "That's all."

"Don't look like that. I don't know who you've been talking to, but whoever it is has been feeding you some bad information. How could I have had a child and you not know about it?"

"I don't know. We go for long stretches of time and don't see each other."

"I'm telling you it's not true. Now close the drapes on your way out," said Carly as she whipped a pillow out from under her head and pulled the sheet over her face.

Kate crossed the room to the windows and pulled the drapes together until just a tiny sliver of light came through the break in the two halves. "I'm going to borrow a car this morning so I can go shopping. My suitcase still hasn't arrived at the airport."

Carly pulled the sheet down to her chin. "What's wrong with my clothes?"

"You're smaller than I am. I can barely breathe in these jeans."

"Unfasten them."

"I did."

"Oh." The wheels of her mind turned. "If that's such a problem, then I'll take you shopping. It'll give us a chance to spend some time together."

"I thought you wanted to sleep."

"Changed my mind. Just give me a few minutes to get ready and we'll go."

"You're sure?"

"Positive. Just don't go anywhere without me."

Kate started to leave.

"Katie?"

She turned back.

"And for heaven's sake, don't tell anyone this crazy story you came to me with. That's all good old Laurel Trent will need to put an end to the wedding."

"All right."

As soon as the door had closed behind Kate, Carly ran to her closet and pulled out a diary she'd hidden at the very back. Taking it to bed with her, she sat cross-legged in the middle of the mattress and turned to the last page she'd written on. While rereading her last entry, she chewed on the end of her pen. Then she began scribbling furiously on a clean page, filling it with her nearly illegible writing.

Things were coming to a head sooner than she'd expected.

Chapter Twelve

Kate went to the kitchen to use the phone there. Mrs. Meredith had already cleaned up after breakfast and was busy somewhere else.

Lifting the receiver from the cradle, Kate pressed the international number for the United States and then her mother's number. The phone at the other end rang six times before it was answered. "Mom," said Kate almost before her mother had finished saying hello, "this is Kate. I'm in England."

"What on earth are you doing there?"

"Visiting Carly." She didn't see any point in telling her about the wedding and hurting her feelings. She'd break it to her when she got back to Chicago.

"And how is your sister?" her mother asked coolly.

"She seems to be fine. Mom, I'm calling because there's something I need to ask you."

"Go ahead."

"Do you know if Carly ever had a child?"

There was silence at the other end.

"Mom?"

"Why do you ask?"

"I can't explain right now. Just trust me that it's important that I find out the truth."

"To my knowledge, your sister has never had a child."

"This would have happened about six or seven years ago, around the same time as my child was born."

"Carly has never had a child. I would have known."

Kate smiled. "Thank you." Relief was evident in her voice.

"What exactly is going on there? Why would you ask me such a question?"

"It's nothing to worry about. Someone told me something, and I wanted to check it out with you. I'm glad it isn't true."

"This person told you that Carly had a child?"

"Among other things."

"Who would say such a thing?"

"Someone who apparently doesn't like Carly for whatever reason. Don't worry about it, Mom. Everything is fine. I'll fill you in completely when I get home."

"When will that be?"

"A week."

"Call me as soon as you get in."

"I will. Goodbye."

As Kate hung up, she looked out the window, which, in a sideways fashion, fronted the cliffs. To her surprise, her sister was walking across the lawn toward the house.

Kate rapped on the window and Carly looked up. With a smile, she waved and walked faster toward a kitchen door that Kate hadn't known was there.

"Katie! There you are. I was just coming to get you," she said as she pushed her windblown hair away from her face. "What are you doing in here?"

"Making a phone call."

"All done?"

"Yes." Kate looked at her sister and tried to imagine her doing what Dee had accused her of. She just couldn't. She was going to take her mother's word for it.

"Are you ready to shop?"

"Sure. I'll get my purse."

"And I have a little surprise for you."

"I think I've had enough surprises for one day."

"You'll like this one. We're taking the boat."

Kate had half risen. She now sat down again. "I don't want to do that, Carly."

"Come on, Katie. I think it's a lovely idea. It'll be fun."

"You know better than anyone how afraid of the water I am."

"And you know what a good swimmer I am. In the unlikely event that you fall overboard, I'll save you," joked Carly.

"That isn't funny."

"We'll save time by going in the boat."

"Time is something I have plenty of."

"I've done it nearly a dozen times without anything bad happening. Besides, I can't take two hours out of my day for driving you around. For heaven's sake, Kate, you're being silly about this. You know I wouldn't let anything bad happen to you."

"Carly..."

"Come on, Katie. It's an adventure. Probably one of our last together for a long time. You'll enjoy it."

Still Kate hesitated.

"Please?"

Kate sighed. She had a bad feeling about it, but let herself be persuaded. After what she'd accused Carly of earlier—and considering how well she was taking it—it was the least Kate could do. "All right, as long as there are life vests."

"Of course there are," said Carly. "Would Gabriel Trent let his daughter get into a boat without them? This is going to be fun. You'll need a sweater or jacket, though, because it's a lot colder on the water than it is on land."

"I don't have one."

"No problem. There are several around here. I'll get a couple and meet you in front."

Kate went to her room to get her purse, then went back downstairs to wait for Carly.

When the door behind her opened, Kate turned around and saw Gabriel walk in. As soon as he saw her, he stopped. "Hello."

It took her a moment to find her voice. "Hello."

He took a step toward her. "Kate?"

"Yes."

His body relaxed before her eyes. "Are you waiting for someone?"

"Carly. We're taking the boat to town."

Gabriel stopped in front of her. "I thought you were afraid of water."

"Carly claims she'll save me if I fall."

"Make sure you wear the life vest."

"I will."

"And be careful. The water's getting a little choppy."

He looked up as Carly started down the stairs and, without saying anything, left the foyer before she reached them.

Why would he do that? wondered Kate. It just wasn't the natural behavior of a man who loved a woman.

Carly snapped her fingers in front of Kate's face. "Hello? What are you so deep in thought about?"

Kate looked at her sister blankly. "I'm sorry. I wasn't paying attention."

Carly handed her a red jacket very much like the one Carly was already wearing. "Here. Put this on."

"Thanks." Kate zipped herself into it as they walked out the door and down the steps.

"Don't look so worried," said Carly. "You're going to enjoy this. Trust me."

They walked across the wide lawn to some steep stone stairs that led to a small boathouse more than a

hundred and fifty feet below. As Kate looked at the boathouse, she saw a flash of movement—a person perhaps. She narrowed her eyes to see who or what it was, but it had disappeared.

The day had turned gray. There was a chill in the damp air that went right through Kate's jacket. The steps were still wet from an earlier rain and a little slick. Slick enough so that Kate had to pay attention to where she put her feet. The moss that had grown on some of the stones made the going a bit more treacherous.

Carly looked over her shoulder at Kate and grinned. "Are you having fun yet?"

"Still waiting."

"It'll get better."

The steps bottomed out at last and flowed into a smooth stone slab that supported a boathouse made of the same stone. The two of them went in through the unlocked door. Carly walked to a lever on the wall and pulled it down. Machinery ground instantly and noisily into motion, and a small boat that had been hoisted almost to the ceiling was slowly lowered into the water, where it bobbed on the waves that flowed in and out through a wooden gate.

Carly hit another switch and the gate was raised. "Ready?" she asked as she climbed down a small, three-step ladder and hopped into the boat.

Kate let out a long breath and went down the ladder with all of the enthusiasm of someone going to certain death. As soon as her feet hit the bottom of the boat and it bobbed, Kate panicked.

Carly pushed down on her shoulders until she was seated securely on a narrow wooden ledge toward the front of the boat. Kate's heart was racing. "Where are the life vests?"

Carly looked around, appearing puzzled. "That's strange. They're usually either in the boat or hanging on the wall. Someone must have taken them to be cleaned. Oh, well."

"Oh, well?" asked Kate.

"Don't be such a worrier. It's a ten-minute ride. What can possibly happen?"

The Gypsy's warning flashed into her mind, but before Kate could react by getting out of the boat, Carly pulled the starter cord on the engine. "You'd think that Gabriel, with all of his money, would invest in a better boat than this," she said. "I'll take care of that once we're married."

It took her three pulls on the black-handled cord to get the engine to respond. Even then, after starting with a roar, it sputtered into silence. Carly gave it another pull. This time it roared to life and remained steady. The noise was deafening as it echoed off the stone walls.

"Here we go," yelled Carly as she guided the boat carefully out to sea, past the rock hazards visible under the water.

Kate hung on to the sides of her wooden seat with such force that her knuckles were white.

Carly, on the other hand, looked right at home, as though she'd made this trip many times before.

"I'm impressed," yelled Kate. "I never knew you had such a seafaring spirit."

Carly grinned at her.

Kate started to relax a little. She kept her body facing her sister at the rear of the boat, but turned her head so she could see where they were going. The cold, salty air stung her cheeks and Kate had to admit that it felt good.

What didn't feel so good was the constant up-and-down motion of the boat over what seemed like huge waves. "It didn't look this rough from up there."

"I know what you mean," called Carly over the noise of the engine. "It never does."

Kate turned her head and looked at the cliffs. She could see the roofline of the house. And there was someone standing along the cliffs, arms akimbo, watching them. Whoever it was was too far away to identify, but Kate had the feeling it was Gabriel. She found that thought somehow comforting.

"How long before we reach the other side?"

"Ten minutes," said Carly. "Maybe fifteen. We're fighting the waves."

When Kate looked back at the cliffs, the lone figure was gone. So was her sense of security. She kept glancing up, but whoever it was never reappeared.

After five minutes, Gabriel's home had come fully into view, but Kate didn't see the village at all. Kate opened her mouth to ask Carly what was going on when the engine made a sputtering noise. It didn't quite die, but came back to life only to sputter and cough again before fading gracelessly into its final silence.

"Oh, great," said Carly.

Kate was still hanging on to the sides of the boat. "What's wrong? Why did the engine die?"

"How should I know? I'm not a mechanic." She pulled the starter cord. Nothing happened.

She pulled it again. Still nothing.

"Maybe if I tried," suggested Kate.

"It won't make any difference. This old thing has no intention of starting."

"So what do we do?" Kate tried to quell her rising panic.

"Wait until someone comes looking for us."

"Which will be when?"

"Soon, probably. People know we're in the boat. When we don't arrive home they'll come looking for us."

"That could be hours." Kate wrapped her arms around herself and looked at the cold, dark water that rocked the boat.

"We'll be fine. Don't worry."

"I know."

Carly looked at her with a quirked brow. "Interesting that this should happen, don't you think? It never has before."

"Meaning?"

Carly shook her head. "Just that it's interesting."

"Are you implying that this is connected to other things that have been happening to you?"

"It could be."

"There's only one hole in that theory."

"Which is?"

"Why would anyone want to frighten you off or even hurt you? What would be the motive?"

"I told you before. There's resistance to the marriage."

Kate shook her head. "I don't buy it."

"You think I'm making the incidents up?"

"No, of course not. They're probably just accidents."

"What about what happened to you in the tower?"

"Like you said before, maybe I was sleepwalking."

"I'm telling you, Kate, someone out there wants me out of the way. And the boat stalling here is just one more example."

Kate looked at her sister for a long moment. As quickly as that, she knew.

Carly grew uneasy. "What's wrong?"

"You are blackmailing Gabriel, aren't you?"

Carly's mouth opened in surprise. "What on earth are you talking about?"

"Willa is yours, isn't she?"

Carly glared at her.

As Kate looked at her sister, she couldn't hide the sympathy in her eyes. "Why didn't you ever tell anyone about the baby? Don't you know that of all of the people in your life, I'm the one who would have understood completely what you went through? What you're still going through?"

"You don't know what you're talking about."

"I could have helped you."

"What could you possibly have done for me?"

"Supported you, just the way you and Mom supported me when I was going through the death of my own child."

Carly looked at her sister and laughed. "Yeah, right."

"I understand that you want your daughter, but this isn't the way to do it."

"Why? Because it isn't your way?"

"What you should do is work out a shared-custody agreement with Gabriel."

"I don't want shared custody."

"You can't take Willa away from Gabriel. He's her father and he loves her. And more importantly Willa loves him. She's happy, healthy and well adjusted."

"You're so far off. This isn't about Willa."

"Then what? Gabriel? You think you can make a life with a man you blackmailed into marriage?"

"I'm sure going to give it my best shot."

"This is crazy. He'll never love you."

Carly angrily twisted the engagement ring off of her finger and flung it at Kate. "Tell me, Katie, is that the kind of ring a man gives a woman he doesn't love?"

She picked up the ring from her lap without looking at it. "If Gabriel gave you this, then yes, it's exactly the kind of ring a man gives a woman he doesn't love."

"He might not now, but he will. As far as he's concerned, I'm the mother of his child. That puts me in a special category."

"And are you Willa's mother?"

Carly looked at Kate, a smile twitching at the corners of her mouth.

The boat suddenly lurched as a large wave rolled under them. Kate jammed Carly's ring on her finger so she wouldn't drop it and grabbed the sides of the boat again. "It's getting rougher."

"Don't worry about it."

Kate felt as though she was going to be ill, but she tried not to show it. "Why won't you talk about Willa?"

"Because you don't need to know all of my secrets. Everything about us is exactly alike except what's on the inside. What's inside me belongs to me."

"Why are you so angry with me?"

"Because you exist."

"That's it?"

"I've spent my life feeling as though I'm in a competition against you. Everything you do, I have to do twice as well."

"No one but you thinks that."

"No one else matters. And you know what? I've succeeded. You work in a museum, I'm a model. You fell in love with Jeff and I got him away from you. And now I'm going to marry Gabriel Trent, and you're eating your heart out because you want him for yourself."

"Do you hear yourself, Carly? Do you hear how sick you sound?"

"I'll tell you something, Kate. I've always resented being a twin. I don't like the fact that there's another one of me on the planet. I'm an original. One of a kind. Being a twin has cramped my style. But I've

managed to break away. If that's sick, then so be it. I revel in my disease.''

The boat rocked violently as a big wave picked it up and let it drop back on the sea. Water sloshed over Kate's shoes. She looked at the floor of the boat where nearly two inches of water had gradually been accumulating, unnoticed by either of its occupants. "Where did this come from?" she yelled, fear in her voice.

Carly reached down and casually trailed her fingers through it. "It looks like we have a leak."

Chapter Thirteen

"What do we do?" asked Kate.

"Try to find the leak."

Their hurtful words forgotten, the two of them got down on their hands and knees and began to feel around in the water for anything that might resemble a fresh flow of water.

Kate moved her hands through the cold water inch by inch as it lapped around her bent knees. The little boat was bombarded by waves, some small and some that nearly knocked her over. "I can't find anything," she called to her sister.

"Neither can I," said Carly. "Keep looking."

But the longer they looked, the deeper the water inside the boat grew.

"We have to start bailing," said Kate. "Help me."

The two of them, their hands cupped, started scooping water out of the boat. It helped a little, but not enough.

Carly suddenly stood up. "I'm going to swim to shore for help."

"No!" yelled Kate. "It's too far."

"Don't be silly. I'm a terrific swimmer, and the waves, as big as they are, will be with me. I'll be back here in no time to get you."

"Carly, please don't."

She smiled. "Bye-bye, Katie." And with that, Carly dove off the side of the boat and disappeared into the waves.

Kate watched frantically for her to surface and relaxed only when Carly's head popped above water and she began to easily stroke her way through the water, the waves, as she had predicted, buoyantly helping to carry her body.

Kate went back to scooping, but the water seemed to be coming in faster now, rapidly replacing the water she managed to get out. She couldn't keep up. The boat was getting lower and lower in the water.

She crawled to the motor, found the starter cord and yanked on it.

The motor didn't even bother to sputter this time.

She pulled on it again.

Nothing.

Again and again she tried, adjusting the choke, jiggling it, hitting it with her hand in frustration. It stayed silent.

The water in the boat was getting too deep to ignore. Kate knew she was going to have to do something because once the boat went down, which looked to be only minutes away, she would be left without anything to hang on to.

A strange calm filled her. She was going to have to do something or die. It was as simple as that. The boat was going to have to be her life preserver until Carly got back with help. And the only way she could use it like that was to overturn it, meaning she was going to have to go into the water and hang on for dear life.

After saying a silent prayer, Kate stood up. The wave action made her unsteady on her feet for a moment, but then she managed to balance herself. Putting her weight on one foot and then the other, she began deliberately rocking the boat back and forth, back and forth, until it was ready to tip over. Then, when she thought it was ready, she put all of her weight on one side. It overturned, just as she expected, but she wasn't able to grab the edge. Instead, she was dumped into the cold water without anything to hold on to.

She had to fight the terror that filled her when the water went over her head. She couldn't breathe. She couldn't even tell which way was up and which was down for several seconds. To Kate, it seemed as though she went down forever, but by kicking her legs, she was able to fight her way to the surface just as she ran out of air. She gulped in water along with air and choked helplessly even as she looked around for the boat.

It was floating upside down perhaps ten feet away. Doing a kind of dog paddle, she was able to get her-

self to the boat and cling to the bottom of it with the upper half of her body.

Wave after wave broke over the boat, covering her completely. But she didn't let go. All she had to do was hang on until Carly came back with help. That's what Kate told herself as the cold gripped her and her arms grew exhausted. Just hang on.

She lost track of time and grew so cold that her entire body shivered uncontrollably.

But she kept hanging on, waiting for Carly to come back for her.

Her arms ached, then went numb, but she refused to let go.

Once, she thought she heard the sound of an engine, but it faded away.

She waited and hoped.

The cold and the waves that kept surging over her head sapped her strength. Little by little, her grip on the boat slipped. She couldn't pull herself up any longer. Her arms and hands wouldn't do what her brain told them. It was as though they belonged to someone else.

Kate realized that she was going to die. This was it. The end of her life.

Her grip slipped further. She sank into the water up to her chin. Then her lips. She didn't have the strength to fight it.

As she resigned herself to her watery grave, the water covered her head. She went under.

Out of nowhere, a hand reached out and grabbed the back of her jacket, yanking her head out of the water.

But for Kate, everything had already gone black.

* * *

The first thing Kate noticed was the antiseptic smell. I must not be dead, thought Kate as she listened to a distant voice paging a doctor. But if she wasn't dead, why couldn't she open her eyes? It was too much effort.

She sensed movement around her. She knew when she was in light and when she was in darkness.

She even thought she heard Gabriel's voice talking to her.

She was just so tired....

Kate opened her eyes. For a time, she stared straight up at the ceiling. Then she started taking in her surroundings. She was in a pretty room with pale striped wallpaper. There were vases of flowers everywhere. A love seat was along one wall and there were comfortable chairs near her bed—next to the dangling IV bottles and tubes.

She turned her head. A man stood in front of the window looking out. "Gabriel?" Her voice was barely a croak, but he heard.

He turned toward the bed. "Where's Kate?"

"What?"

"What did you do to her?"

"I don't know what you're talking about."

He stood over her, his eyes filled with anger. "She's gone and it's your doing. You're going to pay for this one way or another."

"This isn't the time," said a woman she hadn't noticed sitting next to the bed. "She's not strong enough."

Gabriel looked at Kate a moment longer, then turned and strode out of the room.

The woman lifted one of Kate's hands in hers. "You're awake at last."

"Jane!" said Kate in surprise. "Where did you come from?"

"Gabriel called the museum after the accident. They mentioned my name. He found me listed in Kate's address book and called me. I wanted to be here for you, of course."

Kate frowned. "What do you mean 'Kate's address book'? You mean mine."

"No, Kate's. He found it when he was going through the few things she brought with her."

"Jane, why are you talking about me like that?"

"Like what?"

"As though you're speaking about me and not to me."

Jane blinked. "I don't—"

"I'm Kate."

Jane leaned in closer and looked at her really hard. "No," she said, shaking her head. "I'm sorry to have to be the one to tell you this, but Kate hasn't been found. She's gone."

"But I didn't . . . I stayed with the boat and I'm here talking to you."

Jane, who had never been close to Carly—by choice—looked at her with suspicious gray eyes. Carly

was always making trouble. "If you're Kate, show me the freckle."

Kate, careful not to dislodge her numerous tubes, lowered the sheet and lifted her hospital gown. There it was. A little heart.

Jane looked at her dearest friend with eyes suddenly flooded with tears and hugged Kate so tightly it was hard to breathe. Then she straightened away from Kate and looked at her again, afraid to believe the evidence of her own eyes. "Oh, my God, I thought you were dead. What happened out there?"

Kate tried to remember. "What day is this?"

"You've been in the hospital for three days."

"Three days?"

"So what happened?"

Kate leaned back against her pillows. "Carly and I were taking the boat to the village so I could buy some clothes. My suitcase still hadn't arrived from the airport. We got about halfway there when the engine died. Then the boat started filling with water. Carly dove into the water and started swimming to shore for help while I stayed with the boat." Kate looked at Jane with stricken eyes. "Didn't she make it?"

Jane took Kate's hand in hers and raised it to her cheek. "I'm sorry, Kate. There's been no sign of her."

"Oh, no. I should never have let her go."

"It's not as though you had a choice."

Kate shook her head as tears streamed down her cheeks.

Jane smoothed her hand comfortingly over Kate's in silence. There wasn't anything she could say.

After a while, Jane took a tissue and wiped Kate's face. "Everyone thinks you're the one who's dead, Kate."

"Why?"

"You had on Carly's engagement ring. Certain assumptions were made based on that."

"So Gabriel thinks I'm Carly?"

"So did I. So does everyone."

"Jane, does anyone know what happened?"

"Apparently the boat sprang a leak."

"Yes, but why? And why did the engine choose that particular trip to break down?"

"It didn't choose, Kate. It's an engine. It just happened."

"Has the boat been examined by authorities?"

"I don't know."

"Can you find out?"

"Sure. What do you want me to ask?"

"If what happened to the engine and the boat was deliberate."

"Deliberate?"

"Carly told me that she thought someone was trying to kill her, but I refused to believe her."

"This isn't making any sense. Why would anyone want to kill Carly? And who?"

"Believe me, there are some very good reasons, but I can't tell you about them. At least not yet. They affect too many people."

Jane patted her arm. Kate clearly wasn't herself and she wasn't making much sense. "Okay. First things

first, though. I need to let people know you're not Carly."

"No!" said Kate suddenly. "No. I don't want anyone but you to know for now. If someone was trying to kill Carly and they find out they succeeded, they won't try again."

"That would seem to me to be a good thing," said Jane.

"Not if we want to find out who it was."

"But you don't even know if that's the case."

Kate looked straight at Jane. "I don't want you to tell anyone I'm Kate until I say it's all right. Promise me."

"Not even your mother?"

"Not even. I'll tell her when I think it's time."

"Kate, I know this isn't the time to speak ill of Carly, but you know as well as I do that she lied all of the time. What if nothing she told you was true?"

"And what if it was?"

Jane sighed. "I don't like this."

"I don't, either, but what choice is there?"

"We could both just go home and forget about this."

"I wouldn't be able to live with myself if I were to leave this business unfinished. I can't walk away."

Jane sighed. "And I wouldn't be able to live with myself if I left you here alone to fend for yourself."

"So you'll stay for a while?"

"A few days."

"What about your bookstore?"

"I left my assistant in charge. I'm sure he can handle things for a little while without me."

"Thank you, Jane."

Jane leaned over and rested her cheek against Kate's. "I'm just so glad you're here. I thought I'd lost you. We've been best friends for so long, it was as though I'd lost a part of myself."

"I love you, too."

As Jane straightened away from her, Kate gave her a pale imitation of her usual smile. "Would you mind leaving me alone for a while?"

"Of course not." She touched Kate's hand. "I'll get myself something from the cafeteria. It's nearly midnight, and I haven't eaten since this morning. Then I suppose I should make some calls to let people know you're awake."

"Don't do that until morning. I'd really like to have some time to adjust before I have to face everyone."

"All right."

Jane's footsteps echoed softly in the room as she walked away and closed the door behind her.

Kate turned her face toward the window and stared blankly into the night. "Oh, Carly," she whispered as tears rolled silently down her cheeks.

Laurel Trent opened the door of her grandson's office and stepped inside. The room was dark except for the light from the dying fire. She saw him standing beside the fireplace, one hand on the mantel, staring into the flickering flames, the other holding a picture—the one taken at the carnival.

With a heavy heart, she crossed the room and put her hand on his arm. "When was the last time you slept?"

"I don't remember."

"You can't go on this way."

"It's not a choice, Grandmother."

"Gabriel, what is it that's tearing at you like this?"

He shook his head.

"All right, you don't want to talk. But when you do, I'm ready to listen."

"Thank you, Grandmother." He managed a half-hearted smile.

Laurel walked across the room to the door, where she stood looking at her grandson. He had aged a decade in less than a week. It broke her heart to see him like this.

She quietly closed the door as she left.

Gabriel went to the built-in bar and poured himself a drink, downing it in one gulp. No matter how much he drank, it didn't numb what he was feeling. He set the glass firmly on his desk and left his office through the French doors to walk to the cliff.

The wind off the sea that night was bitingly cold, but he didn't notice. All he could think about was that Kate was out there somewhere. She was gone. He would never see her again.

A woman he'd known for a few days had died, and it felt like the end of the world.

Chapter Fourteen

The next day, Kate was sitting on the edge of her hospital bed waiting for someone to pick her up and take her back to Cliff House when Gabriel walked in.

Her heart hammered. If Carly was murdered, Gabriel was the one with the motive.

"Is that all you have?" he asked, inclining his head toward a small suitcase.

"Yes."

He grabbed it by the handle. "Let's go."

She rose from the edge of the bed, still a little unsteady, and fell into step behind him, trying unsuccessfully to keep up. "Wait!"

Gabriel turned around.

"I can't walk that fast."

He waited for her to catch up, but still didn't offer her a helping hand as they went down a floor in the main elevator and walked through the lobby.

His car was in front of the hospital. Gabriel opened the passenger door and reluctantly helped her into the seat. He was as cold and distant as a man could be.

They drove for a few miles, but Gabriel pulled the car to the side of the road and turned the engine off.

"What are you doing?" asked Kate.

"I want to talk to you."

"You could have done that in the hospital."

Gabriel turned in his seat toward her. His eyes were dark with anger. "What happened in that boat?"

Kate pressed her back against the door. "You know as much as I do."

"I want to hear it from you."

"The engine stopped. The boat started leaking."

"Where were the life vests?"

His anger was frightening her. "There weren't any."

"Why not? Who removed them?"

"I don't know."

"What did you do to Kate?"

"Nothing! I did nothing to her!"

Gabriel erupted from the driver's seat and slammed the door after him. He wanted to hurt her.

As Kate watched, partly in fear, partly in fascination, Gabriel strode away from the car and didn't stop until he was fifty yards away. Then he stopped walking and just stood there, his back to the car.

After a time, Gabriel, his hands deep in his pockets, walked back to the car and got in. Without speaking to

Kate, he started the engine. The tires spun and spit gravel as he pulled away from the side of the road onto the road itself.

Kate leaned back in her seat and discreetly studied Gabriel's profile. He looked exhausted.

"The wedding is in two days," said Gabriel suddenly. "Do you still want to go through with it?"

Kate didn't know what to say. What would Carly have said? And she had Willa to consider.

"Well?"

"Yes, I suppose so."

"I should have assumed that. You're not the type to go through a mourning period, even for your sister."

That stung. "You don't know anything about me."

"Believe me, Carly, I know more than I ever wanted to."

Kate stared out the window, tears burning the backs of her eyes.

"If it meets with your approval," said Gabriel, sounding as though he didn't care whether it did or not, "I'd like to change it from a wedding with guests to a private ceremony. It seems appropriate under the circumstances."

"That's fine," said Kate quietly.

He parked the car in front of Cliff House, got out and walked around to the passenger side to open her door.

As she turned in her seat to climb out, their eyes met. Gabriel's were cold and hard. It was as though he were looking through her rather than at her.

It made her heart literally ache, both for him and for Carly. However badly she went about it, this was the man Carly had picked to spend the rest of her life with, and the eyes looking back at her were filled with hate. This was what Carly had seen. How desperate must she have been to do what she'd done?

How desperate was he?

"I'll put your bag in your room," said Gabriel as he walked away from her and up the stairs. "Your sister's friend Jane is across the hall from you."

Kate stood in the foyer feeling a little lost, not quite sure what she should do.

Richard passed his brother on the stairs, ignored him and made straight for Kate. Picking her up in a bear hug, he swung her around. "It's good to see you, Carly!"

Kate couldn't help laughing as he set her back on the ground. "Thank you."

Richard's own smile faded. "Sorry about your sister."

"I know."

"And I know I should have come to see you at the hospital, but places like that give me the creeps."

"It's all right."

"Good. I thought you'd be mad at me." He tweaked her cheek. "You're certainly mellower than I've ever seen you before."

Kate had to remember that she was supposed to be Carly. "It's the new me."

"I like it. Keep it up." He looked at his watch. "Gotta go. Will I see you later?"

"I'll be here."

He kissed her forehead.

Kate went up the stairs and headed for her room. She was nearly there when she realized that Carly's room was now her room. She had to retrace a few steps.

Standing in front of her sister's door, Kate hesitated for a moment, then pushed down on the handle and went inside.

Carly's perfume still hung in the air.

Kate closed the door behind her, then slowly walked around the room, stopping in front of the dresser to touch her sister's hairbrush, lipstick and jewelcase.

She went to the window and looked out at the sea. Tears stung her eyes, but she forced them back. First she'd find out who was responsible for what happened and then she'd cry.

There was a tap on the door.

"Come in."

Jane crossed the room to Kate and gave her a hug. "I bet it's nice to be out of the hospital."

"Very."

"Just so you know, the airline sent your lost luggage over. I had them put the suitcase in your room, but thought you might want your own clothes, so I put the folded things in the second and third dresser drawers and hung the rest in the closet in here."

"Thanks, Jane, but if I'm going to pretend I'm Carly, I'll have to wear her clothes."

"Of course."

"So what do we do now?"

"I'm not sure." Kate sat on the edge of the bed. "I'm supposed to marry Gabriel the day after tomorrow."

"You're not, of course."

"I will if I have to."

"Why?"

She took Jane's hand and pulled her onto the bed beside her. "There are some things I have to tell you, and you have to give me your word that you won't tell anyone else."

"You have it, of course."

"Have you met Willa?"

Jane smiled. "I have. She's a charmer."

"She's also Carly's daughter."

Jane's mouth dropped open. "What?"

"Carly was blackmailing Gabriel into marriage by threatening him. If there was no marriage, she told him she was going to take him to court to get custody of Willa."

Jane stared at her for a long moment. "So you're saying that Gabriel had a reason for killing Carly."

"The best."

"Do you think he's capable of doing something like that?"

"He hates her, Jane. I've seen it in his eyes, heard it in his voice. The answer is yes, I think to protect someone he loves, he's capable of murder."

Jane shivered.

"There's also Richard."

"What about him?"

"Carly has been teasing him for months. He brought her here as his guest and she ended up engaged to his brother."

"That's quite a shot to the ego."

"Exactly."

"So you have two who might have done it."

"And whoever else knows about Willa and Carly, including Gabriel's attorney, Harry Granville and his wife."

"The plot thickens. Of course, the answer could be that no one did it and it was just an accident."

"Believe me, I hope that is the answer."

"How exactly do you plan to find out?"

"By being Carly and making Gabriel go through with the marriage. Whoever killed Carly thinks they made a mistake and killed me. I think they'll come after Carly again and finish the job."

"How can you protect yourself against something like that?"

"I'm already protected by the simple fact that I know what's going on. I won't trust anyone."

"Don't you think you should bring the police in on this?"

"This is a small, sparsely populated area. I have no way of knowing how close they are to Gabriel. If I go to them, they might in turn tell him, and then where would I be?"

"I suppose you have a point."

"Did you call them about the boat?"

"Yes, just a little while ago."

"What did they say?"

"They couldn't tell whether anything was tampered with or not. The motor stopped because a spark plug apparently fell out. And as for the leak, there was a hole in the bottom of the boat that could be the result of bumping on something."

"That's no help."

"Who knew you were going out in the boat?"

"Gabriel."

"That's it?"

"That's it. Unless Carly said something when I wasn't around. And I saw a flash of someone near the stairs leading to the boathouse as Carly and I were walking toward it."

"Couldn't you see who it was?"

"I think it was Gabriel."

"I don't like this, Kate. Not one bit. I think you should just pack your things and go home."

"I can't leave Willa. And I can't leave this thing with Carly unfinished. I need for you to do me another favor."

"Just ask."

"Call my mother and tell her the truth. I don't feel right about keeping her in the dark. She shouldn't have to mourn two daughters. Just make sure she understands that she's not to say anything to anyone else."

"I will." Jane sighed as she shook her head. "Oh, Katie, I have a bad feeling about this. A very bad feeling."

Things were getting down to the wire. Kate wasn't sure she could go through with the wedding, didn't

know if she should. If Gabriel had wanted to harm her, he'd had plenty of opportunity since she'd gotten out of the hospital.

She watched him with his grandmother, watched him with his daughter. He wasn't a murderer. How could she ever have thought that of him?

But somebody was. Carly had known it, and Kate hadn't taken her seriously.

And the Gypsy had known it, too. Everything she'd spoken of had come to pass.

Kate looked at her watch. Nearly midnight—the night before the wedding. Her stomach was tied in knots. She couldn't sleep. She needed to get away from the house; needed to think.

Taking Carly's keys from her drawer, Kate left her room and went outside to Carly's car, got in and took off. She had no destination in mind, just somewhere else.

Anywhere else.

If she left Cliff House now, she'd never find out what had happened to her sister. And if she told people who she really was, no one would have a reason to make another attempt on her life. His—or her—work would be finished and they could just fade away without anyone ever knowing that they were the one who murdered her sister.

Kate couldn't just leave things like that. She had to know.

And Willa.

Kate didn't know what to do or how to behave toward her. No one had told her that the woman she

knew as Kate was dead. As far as Willa was concerned, Kate had had to go back to Chicago and the woman still here was Carly. The child was polite enough to her, but there wasn't the warmth there had been between them when Kate was Kate.

And Kate hadn't wanted to create that warmth again because this time, as Carly, it would have been a lie—a noticeable lie. Everyone would have noticed the change in behavior, no one more so than Gabriel.

She was so afraid of losing Willa completely. Kate loved the child as much as if Willa were her own. Kate's world lit up every time Willa walked into the room. What would happen when Gabriel found out she wasn't Carly? That she'd lied?

As Kate sped along in the dark silence in the little red convertible, the bitingly cold wind whipped her hair furiously. She made the hairpin turns at speeds more like Carly than herself, zigzagging right and left, never far from the edge of the cliffs.

She was rounding one when she heard a pop. The car lurched out of control, but Kate fought to keep it on the road, her foot jamming the brake pedal.

The car slid to a stop on the gravel shoulder less than two feet from the drop.

Kate, her hands still gripping the steering wheel, sat back in her seat, her breathing ragged, her heart hammering. She was as still as a statue.

And then the tears began to fall, silently rolling down her cheeks until there were no more.

She was as unhappy as she'd ever been, and she couldn't see the end.

Taking a few deep breaths, Kate wiped the backs of her hands over her wet cheeks and climbed out of the car. It listed to one side. The left rear tire had blown out.

She reached into the glove compartment and pressed the trunk button. It popped open and she went around to look for a spare tire.

There wasn't one.

She closed it, raised the neck of her sweater and started walking.

Kate looked at herself in the mirror. She was wearing Carly's wedding gown. Because she'd lost weight in the hospital, it fit perfectly. The creamy satin dress had something of a bustier top that fit her upper body like a glove and gathered momentum from the waist down, gradually adding yards and yards of material. There was a beautifully worked lace overlay that covered her otherwise bare shoulders and had a design that showed off Kate's elegant neck.

Jane walked in and smiled. "How are you doing?"

"All right."

"Are you sure you want to do this?"

"Not at all."

"It's not too late to back out."

"If I do, I'll never find out who killed Carly."

"Maybe no one did, Kate. Maybe it was just an accident."

"I don't think so, Jane. There were just too many accidents."

"All right," she said as she fussed with Kate's sophisticated French twist, "but I think you're making a mistake. Anyway, I think it was wise of you to eliminate the bridesmaids and cancel the reception afterward, considering all that's gone on."

"That was Gabriel's idea."

Their eyes met in the mirror. "Kate, he strikes me as being a good man."

"I know."

"If he didn't murder Carly, what you're doing to him is unforgivable."

"I know that, too."

"If you and he ever had a chance to make it through life together, this will ruin it."

"Why would you think I'd want Gabriel for myself?"

"It's in your eyes every time you look at him. If you aren't in love, then I don't know what love is."

Kate looked stricken. "I didn't realize it was so obvious."

"Maybe only to me, because I love you so much."

Kate turned and hugged her. "I'm so glad you're here."

"Me, too. I only hope I'll be around when the truth comes out and we have to pick up the pieces of what's left of your life."

She picked up the veil from the bed and carefully arranged it on Kate's head. Stepping back, she looked at her handiwork. "You look stunning."

"The irony is that I usually hated Carly's taste, but this wedding dress is exactly the one I would have chosen."

There was a loud knock on the door, and then Richard walked in unceremoniously, dressed in his finest. "The music is starting. Are you ready?"

Kate took a deep breath. "As ready as I'll ever be."

"Let's do it."

When they got to the top of the stairs, Kate could hear the strains of the wedding march. She started to tremble. Richard covered her hand with his. "It's going to be all right."

She smiled at him, and together they started down the stairs.

The few guests still invited were in a living room where the furniture had been arranged to make room for a small wedding party. Flowers were tastefully arranged. They had eliminated all of the trappings of a wedding, including the flower girl. Willa, dressed in a white chiffon dress with a pink ribbon at her waist, sat with her grandmother. The Granvilles were there, along with some other people Kate didn't know but Carly probably did.

Gabriel, darkly handsome in his tuxedo, stood facing forward, away from Kate, as Richard walked Kate down the aisle that had been formed by the chairs.

As she stood beside him, Kate glanced at his taut profile. He was angry and unyielding. She couldn't blame him.

Kate tried to focus on what the minister was saying, but she couldn't. She couldn't focus on anything ex-

cept that she shouldn't be here, in this dress with this man. It wasn't right. She was going to have to figure out some other way to discover what had really happened to Carly.

She raised her hand and put it on Gabriel's arm. "I can't do this," she whispered.

He looked at her for the first time. "What?"

"I can't do this."

The minister had moved on, passing the point where he asked for any objections.

There was a commotion in the foyer. A woman's voice was raised. Then there were the sounds of footsteps running, growing louder.

"This has to stop immediately!"

Kate turned to find her mother standing breathlessly in the doorway.

"Thank God I've come in time."

"Who are you?" asked Gabriel.

Jacqueline Fairfax looked right at Kate. "Her mother."

All color drained from Harry Granville's face. He knew with the certainty of the guilty what was about to happen. He leaned forward and touched Laurel Trent on the shoulder. "Get Willa out of here now."

Without asking questions, she took Willa by the hand and walked quickly from the room.

Kate's mother moved closer. "Why don't you tell the man next to you who you really are?"

"Mother—"

"You tell him or I will."

Kate lifted the veil from her face and looked at Gabriel. "I'm Kate, not Carly."

How he managed it was a miracle, but his expression didn't change. "What?"

"Carly died when the boat sank, not me."

She could see him swallow hard. He reached out with a shaking hand and touched her face. "You're my Kate?"

"I'm so sorry."

And then his mouth tightened. "You let me— You watched all of us mourning for you, and you allowed it. Why?"

"I thought someone here was responsible for Carly's death. You all assumed I was Carly, so I just let it continue. I didn't know any other way to find out who murdered her. I'm so sorry."

His eyes moved over her face. There was joy there mixed with an anger that was so real it burned her.

Her mother moved toward her. "Katie, there's more."

She turned back to her mother and waited.

"Willa isn't Carly's child."

Harry Granville rose suddenly. "Really, I don't think this is the time to air all of this."

"Sit down, Harry," said Gabriel. "Let the woman talk."

Jacqueline remained undistracted, her eyes on her daughter. "Willa is your baby."

Kate thought she must have misheard. "What?"

"Your baby was born alive. Carly pretended to be you and signed her over to Mr. Granville for adoption by the Trents."

Kate felt as though she'd taken a blow to the stomach. "Why would she do that? And why would you let her?"

"I thought it would be best for you. There you were, nineteen and unmarried. You wanted to finish college, but I knew you never would with a baby to take care of. I certainly didn't want to take care of another child. So before you had the baby, I made inquiries about adoption possibilities. An attorney I had contacted got in touch with Mr. Granville, who in turn got in touch with me."

Kate couldn't believe what she was hearing. "You had no right...."

"You had already told me you wouldn't consider adoption," said her mother, "even though it was the right thing to do. What kind of life could you have provided for that child?"

"It was my decision to make. And for you to tell me she was dead! My God, Mother, what were you thinking?"

"Carly agreed with me. Having a child at that point would have ruined your life."

Gabriel looked at his longtime friend. "Is this true, Harry?"

"I'm afraid so."

"Did you know that Carly wasn't Willa's natural mother?"

Harry couldn't lie any longer. "I knew. I've known all along. But what you have to understand, Gabriel, is the kind of position I was in. I knew how much you and Stephanie wanted a child. We'd been through the normal channels and the waiting lists were years long. This opportunity fell in my lap."

"Where did the money go?"

"I gave the entire fifty thousand dollars to Kate's mother."

Kate couldn't swallow, her throat was so closed. "You took money for my baby? You sold my child?"

"I needed it, Katie. Your father had left me with nothing. Everything I had went into raising you and Carly. There was nothing left for me. So after Carly signed the papers, I gave her half of the money and kept the other half for myself."

"The people at the hospital, did they know?"

"One nurse did. She thought we were doing the right thing, so she helped us by keeping other people away from you. We told them you were having problems dealing with the adoption and asked them not to mention it to you. And you were so lost in your grief that you weren't speaking to anyone."

"But my doctor..."

"When he thought he was speaking to you about the baby, he was in fact speaking to Carly. That's why we spirited you out of the hospital so quickly. Carly took your place. She refused the final physical exam and they released her with no one the wiser."

"And my baby's grave?"

"Empty."

Kate shook her head. "How could you?"

"Oh, Katie," said her mother as she moved toward her. "I'm so sorry. I see now that it was a terrible thing to do, but at the time I thought it was best for you."

"You took money. You sold my child, your grandchild. And you're sorry? I lost six years of my daughter's life, I grieved for six long years, and you're sorry?" Kate was filled with a rage like none she had ever felt before.

Her mother reached out to touch her hand.

Kate jerked hers back. "Don't touch me. Don't speak to me ever again. Just get out of my life."

"Katie," her mother pleaded with tears streaming down her face, "I love you. Everything I did was for you. Don't turn your back on me now."

Kate took a deep breath. "From this moment forward, you're dead to me."

Lifting her skirts, Kate ran from the room. Jane rose to go after her friend, but first stopped in front of Jacqueline Fairfax and looked at her with all of the disgust that was in her. "You unspeakable woman."

Gabriel's rage was deep as he looked at Harry Granville. "I want you out of my house now. Don't ever come back."

"Gabriel, you have to listen to me. It isn't the way it sounds."

"Get out, Harry."

Then he looked at Kate's mother, distraught and not knowing what to do. "I'll arrange for your transportation back to the airport."

With that, he moved past her and through the door.

Chapter Fifteen

Kate stood near the edge of the cliff holding her jacket closed against the wind. Carly was out there somewhere.

"Hello, Katie."

Her heart caught. It couldn't be. She turned slowly and found herself looking into the eyes of her twin. "Carly!" she said, shock clearly ringing in her voice.

Kate started to go to her, but Carly held up a gun in both hands and pointed it at her. "Stay where you are, Katie."

"What are you doing?"

"Eliminating one of us. I told you before that I don't like being a twin. You were supposed to die when I pushed you over the railing, but you didn't. Then you

were supposed to die when the boat sank, but you didn't do that, either. Even the flat tire didn't work. So it looks like you're going to have to die here. And this time I'll stick around to make sure the job gets finished.''

Kate couldn't believe what she was hearing. ''That was you? It was all you?''

''All me,'' she said proudly.

''Why? Why would you do it? Do you hate me so much?''

''You have no idea. You never have. I've wanted you dead since we were children, although I have to admit you were more useful to me then than you are now.''

''What did I ever do to you?''

''You existed, Katie. There we were, looking exactly alike, and for some reason people always seemed to like you better. Jane wanted to be your friend, but not mine. Jeff loved you instead of me. Do you know that even Gabriel fell in love with you? I couldn't believe it when I saw him looking at you. He hated me and fell in love with you. It boggles the mind. And, of course, with me presumably out of the way, you're free to love him back. Quite a happy little ending for you.''

Kate inclined her head toward the gun. ''What's that all about?''

''You have to die. Of course, it won't really be you. It'll be Carly. Carly, not dead after all, but bent on murdering poor Kate. No one will feel any sympathy for you. You'll get what you deserve. And I'll be left. I'll become you. Gabriel will love me because he'll think I'm you.''

"You're a little behind on your information. Gabriel doesn't want anything to do with me."

"Don't even try that, Kate."

"I'm serious. I lied to him. In an ironic twist that you might enjoy, I allowed him to believe that I was you after the accident. I was wearing your engagement ring, so it was easy enough to get away with it."

"Why would you do that?"

"Because I thought someone had murdered you, and he seemed the most likely to have done it. I decided that if Gabriel believed he'd failed, he'd try again, and then I'd have him red-handed."

Carly smiled. "This is delicious. How did he find out the truth?"

"I was ready to go through with the marriage as you, but before I could, Mom arrived and told him the truth."

"Good old Mom. So you know about Willa?"

Kate nodded. "She's mine."

"That's right."

"How could you take her away from me? How could you lie to me like that?"

"Katie, Katie, Katie. I'm standing here with a gun pointed at you and you're wondering how I could have given your baby away? She was your child with the man I loved. I didn't want you anywhere near her. The money was an added bonus. Mom took half and I took the other half. It paid the bills when I first went to New York to kick off my modeling career. I suppose I should thank you."

Kate's throat was so tight she could barely swallow.

"Don't worry about Gabriel, though. I'll charm him into forgiving you. Of course, it'll be me he's forgiving."

"He'll know."

"How?"

"Because we're different."

Carly smiled. "Nice try." She waved the gun. "Move closer to the edge."

"No."

She took a threatening step toward Kate. "I said move closer to the edge, or I'll shoot you and throw you over myself."

Kate took a small step back.

"Go back farther."

"Carly, this is insane. You don't want to do this."

"I've never wanted anything more. It's been clear to me for years that one of us has to die, and it isn't going to be me."

"We're sisters."

"Bye, Katie. Now jump."

The wind whipped Kate's hair as she looked down. It was a long fall. "I can't."

"You either jump or I'll shoot you. You know I won't miss from three feet away. I guess the question you have to answer is if you'd rather take your chances with the gun or the cliff." Her tone of voice was perfectly reasonable. If one didn't listen to the words, it would have sounded like a normal conversation.

Kate saw a movement from the corner of her eye, but she didn't dare look for fear of alerting Carly.

"Do it, Katie. Now."

Kate could see her start to squeeze the trigger, but there was no way she was going to jump.

Someone suddenly tackled Carly from the side. A loud explosion filled the air and Kate felt herself being knocked back by the force of the bullet that hit her arm.

Because Carly was so close to Kate when Gabriel hit her, he was able to grab Kate's hand and yank her back to safety before she went over.

Carly was quick. She was on her feet with the gun before Gabriel could get back to her. He immediately pushed Kate behind him and began backing away from the cliff.

"Isn't that touching?" said Carly as she circled. "She lies to you and still you protect her."

"Put down the gun, Carly," said Gabriel.

She smiled. "I don't think so."

"It's over."

"Certainly things haven't worked out the way I wanted them to, but it's hardly over." She motioned with her gun. "Come here, Katie."

Gabriel held Kate tightly against his back.

"Katie," she said in a singsong voice. "Either you come here or I'll shoot him."

Kate started to move, but Gabriel's grip tightened. "No," he said. "If you want her, you're going to have to go through me."

"You think I won't?" The wind was really strong. Carly had to keep pushing her hair out of her face with her free hand.

A gust hit all of them, nearly knocking Gabriel and Kate both off balance. Carly screamed and stumbled—and then disappeared.

Gabriel ran forward, but there was nothing he could do. He saw her body hit the rocks more than a hundred and fifty feet below. He caught Kate in his arms and pressed her face in his shoulder. "Don't look. It's not something you need to see."

He could feel silent sobs shaking her shoulders.

"As you grieve, Kate, remember that she ended up where she would have sent you."

"I know. But she's my sister."

He held Kate tightly and pressed his lips against the top of her head. "All that matters to me is that you're all right. I couldn't have survived losing you twice."

She looked up at him.

Gabriel gave her a gentle smile as he cupped her face in his hands and moved his thumbs over her tear-stained cheeks. "Let's go back to the house."

Kate nodded and moved under the shelter of his protective arm as they walked.

Gabriel accompanied Kate, her mother and Carly's body back to Chicago. He took charge of things that were too painful for them to deal with.

As they stood at her grave site on a crisp fall morning, Kate and her mother said their last goodbyes while Gabriel waited for them in the background.

He placed his hand in the middle of Kate's back as they walked to the limousine. All three sat in silence as

the driver put it into gear and the black car made its smooth way toward the city.

They stopped at Jacqueline Fairfax's small house first. Kate didn't look as her mother got out.

"Katie," she said in a thick voice, "I'm so sorry about everything. If I could take it all back, I would. I never meant to hurt you or Carly."

"Goodbye," said Kate emotionlessly. She would not, could not, forgive her mother. This was the last time they would ever see each other.

The older woman stepped away, and the driver shut the door. A moment later, they were gliding along again toward Kate's apartment.

Gabriel watched her lovely, sad face. They hadn't had a chance to talk. It never seemed to be the right time. And Kate had been so lost in her thoughts.

When the car stopped in front of her building and the driver opened the door, she turned to Gabriel. "I'd like you to come upstairs. There are some things we need to discuss."

He followed her out of the car, into the building and up to the tenth floor on the elevator.

Her apartment was the way he would have expected it to be: sparsely furnished, but with beautiful things. She probably bought pieces as she could afford them.

"May I get you some coffee?" she asked stiffly as she finished hanging her coat in the foyer closet.

"No, thank you."

She went into the living room and sat in a beautiful but uncomfortable-looking chair. "Please," she said, waving him onto the couch.

"I'll stand."

Kate rubbed her forehead. "Look," she said tiredly, "I know you must rue the day you ever met a Fairfax. We've made your life a living hell. I've done a lot of thinking about Willa and I've decided that I won't do anything to try to take her away from you. As far as she's concerned, you're her father. It would be devastating to her to suddenly lose you." Her eyes met his. "But I also think I have something to contribute to her life. She doesn't have to know I'm her mother if you think it's best that she not be told. But I'd like to be able to spend some time with her. Maybe she could come here during her Christmas vacation, or I could visit her. Whatever you'd be comfortable with."

"Are you finished?"

She nodded.

"This has been quite a week for uncovering the truth. Mine, as well as yours." He sat on the table in front of her so that they were eye level. "I love you, Kate. I think I must have from the moment you first smiled at me. There was something in you that touched me more deeply than I've ever been touched by a woman. I was upset when I found out you were pretending to be Carly, but not for the reasons you thought." He took her hands in his. "I was upset because I went through hell thinking you were dead. It was the worst time of my life, and you could have prevented it with just a few words."

"I did to you what my mother and sister did to me. I'm so sorry."

"I know that." He raised her hands to his lips. "I know. And we're past that now." He looked into her eyes. "Kate, I love you so much I ache with it. I can't leave you here. I want you to come back to England with me—as my wife."

Kate's eyes filled with tears.

"What's this?" he asked gently.

"I didn't want to love you. I've tried so hard not to. But it wasn't any use. Even when I thought you might have had something to do with the boat sinking and Carly's supposed drowning, I couldn't shake my feelings for you. I hated myself for it."

"And now?"

"Oh, Gabriel." Her voice caught. "I didn't know this kind of love was possible. You fill my heart and soul. I don't ever want to be separated from you."

"Then I take it your answer to my proposal is yes?" She nodded.

He rose from the table and opened his arms. "Come here."

She moved into them as though she'd always belonged there. Gabriel held her close. "You feel so good," he said above her ear.

"Stay with me," she said.

"Are you sure?"

She nodded into his shoulder, then leaned back and looked into his eyes. "I need you tonight, Gabriel, like I've never needed anyone before."

He cupped her face in his hands and lowered his mouth to hers, kissing her with more tenderness than passion. Kate needed his tenderness.

When he raised his head, she looked into his eyes and saw how much he loved her. She took him by the hand and led him to her bedroom.

She started to undress herself, but Gabriel took her hands in his. "Don't."

He picked her up in his arms and gently laid her on the bed. Lying beside her, he pulled her into his arms and held her for a long time; just held her. He could feel the tension draining from her body as he lightly stroked her hair and back.

With a finger under her chin, he raised her face to his and kissed her for a long time. Her lips were so responsive.

He kissed her more deeply as his hand began to skillfully undo her blouse button by button. He slid it from her shoulders and dropped it onto the floor. Her skirt joined it a moment later, along with his shirt.

When Kate tried to touch him, Gabriel caught her hand in his and looked down at her. "No, my sweet Kate. Just lie here. Let me love you tonight. Close your eyes and let your body relax."

Kate hadn't been with a man since she was nineteen years old. She didn't know if it was possible to relax, but she tried.

He started with her mouth, caressing her lips with his, moving over her throat and the gentle swell of her breasts, all the time gently stroking her with his hand.

He drew his tongue teasingly over her nipples, circling them and then gently sucking first one and then the other.

Kate could feel her blood pulsing through her veins. All of her senses were heightened. She tried to touch him again, but he caught her hand in his and held it as his mouth moved over her flat stomach, going lower.

Kate's breath came in short gasps. Just as his tongue found its mark, Kate started crying. "No. I can't."

"Shh," said Gabriel as he pressed her back onto the pillows, his mouth gently caressing the warm skin of her stomach, moving upward between her breasts until his lips found hers. "It's all right," he whispered.

"I'm sorry."

"There's nothing to be sorry about. I love you, and that means waiting until you're ready. I want you to come to me when you can do it without reservation and without tears. I'll wait as long as it takes. You just rest now. Tomorrow I'm taking you back to England."

Kate raised her head and looked down at him. "Are you sure you want me? You aren't doing this just because of Willa, are you?"

"Oh," he said with a smile, "I want you." He took her hand in his and placed it on his very erect self. "I want you like I've never wanted anyone. It has nothing to do with Willa." He pressed her head back onto his shoulder. "You get some sleep, Kate. I'll be right here when you wake up. Everything that's happened until now will seem like a bad dream. You'll see."

Gabriel parked the car in front of Cliff House and walked around to the passenger door to let Kate out.

She put her hand in his and looked up at him. "I'm nervous," she said.

"About what?"

"Seeing Willa. What if she doesn't want me for her mother?"

"Let's go inside and talk to her before you start worrying about it."

As they approached the house hand-in-hand, Willa came flying out the front door and raced toward them. "Mommy!" she yelled as she threw herself into Kate's arms.

Kate held her daughter in her arms, her tear-filled eyes meeting Gabriel's. "How?" she asked.

"Grandmother told her last night."

"Thank you."

He leaned over and kissed her. "Welcome home, my dear Kate."

Epilogue

Kate opened her eyes. The bedroom was dark. Turning her head slightly, she looked at the clock—2:00 a.m. She didn't have to reach out to see if Gabriel was sleeping beside her. She knew he wasn't. She always knew when he was near and when he was not.

Slipping out from under the covers, she left their room and went barefoot downstairs to his office. Gabriel was standing in front of his window, staring outside.

Kate came up behind him and wrapped her arms around his waist, resting her cheek on his back.

He closed his eyes and covered her hands with his. "I love you, Kate."

She smiled. "Then come to bed and show me how much."

He turned around and pulled her into his arms. "Today has been a strange day. I keep going over and over all of the things that led us to where we are at this moment."

"Is it because today is Willa's birthday?"

"I think so. I can't get what you must have gone through out of my mind. I don't ever want you to have another unhappy moment."

A gentle smile curved her mouth, and she raised her hand to his handsome face. "As long as our children are healthy and you keep loving me, I won't."

Gabriel kissed her with lingering tenderness. "And how is our newest creation this evening?"

Kate touched her stomach, just beginning to show signs that there was a life within. "Sleeping soundly, I think."

"Do you feel all right?"

"More than all right."

His eyes moved over her face. "I'm so lucky to have found you. I can't imagine what my life would have been like if you hadn't come into it. We nearly missed each other completely. It's only by a twist of fate here and a twist there that we came together."

Kate undid the first button of his shirt and placed a kiss there.

Then she undid the second button and kissed him there.

Her lips followed her hands down to his belt as she unbuckled it.

Gabriel groaned and went down on his knees, pulling his wife into his arms and kissing her deeply and thoroughly.

He lifted her nightgown up and ran his fingers over her smooth skin, down her back, over her hips. He pulled her nightgown off the rest of the way and tossed it aside. His shirt and pants joined it.

Gabriel laid Kate gently on the floor and looked at her with such love in his eyes that it made her ache in response.

His body half covered hers as he kissed her again. His lips moved over her body lingeringly, his tongue bringing her to vibrant life.

He rested his cheek on her abdomen. "Are you sure we won't hurt the baby?"

"I'm sure," she said with a smile. "The doctor said it was all right."

Gabriel moved on top of her, entering her gently.

Kate wrapped her legs around him and kissed his ear. "I won't break," she whispered.

His mouth came down on hers. Their bodies moved as one, Gabriel thrusting deep inside her and Kate meeting him with every movement until they both exploded.

Out of breath and still inside her, Gabriel raised his head and gazed into her eyes. He kissed the corners of her mouth; he kissed her eyelids and her damp hair. Then he wrapped her in his arms and held her to him as though he'd never let her go.

Kate buried her face in his neck and kept herself wrapped around his body, holding him inside of her.

There was no more guilt. She wouldn't live her life that way. The past was the past, and all the mess that went with it could stay there. This was her life now: the man she loved more than life itself and the daughter she thought she'd lost forever. Now there was a new child on the way. A child of their love. A little brother or sister for Willa. Things had come full circle.

Gabriel looked down at her and smiled, and Kate's heart sang in joy.

* * * * *

Silhouette®

Take 4 bestselling love stories FREE

Plus get a FREE surprise gift!

Special Limited-time Offer

Mail to Silhouette Reader Service™

3010 Walden Avenue
P.O. Box 1867
Buffalo, N.Y. 14240-1867

YES! Please send me 4 free Silhouette Special Edition® novels and my free surprise gift. Then send me 6 brand-new novels every month, which I will receive months before they appear in bookstores. Bill me at the low price of $3.34 each plus 25¢ delivery and applicable sales tax, if any.* That's the complete price and a savings of over 10% off the cover prices—quite a bargain! I understand that accepting the books and gift places me under no obligation ever to buy any books. I can always return a shipment and cancel at any time. Even if I never buy another book from Silhouette, the 4 free books and the surprise gift are mine to keep forever.

235 BPA A3UV

Name	(PLEASE PRINT)	
Address	Apt. No.	
City	State	Zip

This offer is limited to one order per household and not valid to present Silhouette Special Edition® subscribers. *Terms and prices are subject to change without notice. Sales tax applicable in N.Y.

Silhouette

SPECIAL EDITION

™

WELCOME TO SILVER CREEK COUNTY

A place full of small-town Texas charm, where
everybody knows your name and falling
in love is all in a day's work!

Award-winning author **SHARON DE VITA** has
spun several delightful stories full of matchmaking
kids, lonely lawmen, single parents and humorous
townsfolk! Watch for the first two books,
THE LONE RANGER
(Special Edition #1078, 1/97)
and
THE LADY AND THE SHERIFF
(Special Edition #1103, 5/97).
And there are many more heartwarming
tales to come!

So come on down to Silver Creek and make
a few friends—you'll be glad you did!

Look us up on-line at: http://www.romance.net

SE-SILV1

Harlequin and Silhouette celebrate
Black History Month with seven terrific titles,
featuring the all-new *Fever Rising*
by Maggie Ferguson
(Harlequin Intrigue #408) and
A Family Wedding by Angela Benson
(Silhouette Special Edition #1085)!

Also available are:
Looks Are Deceiving by Maggie Ferguson
Crime of Passion by Maggie Ferguson
Adam and Eva by Sandra Kitt
Unforgivable by Joyce McGill
Blood Sympathy by Reginald Hill

On sale in January at your favorite
Harlequin and Silhouette retail outlet.

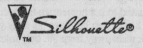